A Simple Story

A Simple Story

Leonardo Sciascia

Translated by Howard Curtis

ET REMOTISSIMA PROPE

Modern Voices

Modern Voices
Published by Hesperus Press Limited
4 Rickett Street, London sw6 1ru
www.hesperuspress.com

First published as *Una storia semplice* in 1989 and *Candido; ovvero,
Un sogno fatto in Sicilia* in 1977

Una storia semplice and *Candido* © Copyright Leonardo Sciascia Estate.
All rights reserved. Published in Italy by Adelphi Edizioni, Milano.
Introduction and English language translation © Howard Curtis, 2010
Foreword © Paul Bailey, 2010

Designed and typeset by Fraser Muggeridge studio
Printed in Jordan by Al-Khayyam Printing Press

ISBN: 978-1-84391-425-9

Contents

Foreword

It would not be too fanciful to describe Leonardo Sciascia, who was born in the Sicilian town Racalmuto in 1921 and died in Palermo in 1989, as a writer worthy of comparison with George Orwell. Like Orwell, he did not confine himself to a specific literary form. He was, by turns, a novelist, a critic, a dramatist, a polemicist and a political commentator with stringently argued views. Sciascia, whose birth coincided with the first serious manifestation of Italian Fascism, had the Orwellian gift for offending politicians of both the extreme Right and the far Left. He was never afraid to express unpopular opinions. To his admirers, he was the conscience of Italy, scenting out corruption in successive governments and the surreal legal system. He was the sharpest thorn in the blemished flesh of Giulio Andreotti, whose numerous misdeeds in high office are chronicled in Paolo Sorrentino's riveting film *Il Divo*. It was Sciascia who chastised the Prime Minister for covering up the truth about Aldo Moro's kidnapping and subsequent murder by the Red Brigade. Many of the questions he raised remain unanswered three decades later.

Leonardo Sciascia's greatest, and most abiding, work is concerned with his native Sicily, the sulphurous island whose people he loved and loathed throughout his life. The Sicilian society he depicts in such novels as *Il consiglio d'Egitto* (*The Council of Egypt*), which deals with a colossal forgery that takes place in eighteenth-century Palermo, and the terrifying *A ciascuno il suo* (translated variously as *A Man's Blessing* and, more accurately, *To Each His Own*) is composed of the gullible, the compromised and the downright wicked. In that second book a Mafia lawyer arranges to have a doctor and a chemist extinguished. A schoolmaster who finds him out is similarly dispatched. The lawyer eventually marries the doctor's widow. This is a classic study of everyday evil, more convincing in its sheer ordinariness than quasi-Romantic tosh like Mario Puzo's *The Godfather*. Sciascia invests the Mafia in his fiction with something akin to the moral authority that was previously the almost sole possession of the Roman Catholic Church. Judges, the police, businessmen, bankers, doctors and even priests bow low before that authority, based as it is on blackmail, threats and money and property illegally, and often brutally, obtained.

The two novellas collected here show Sciascia at his mordantly ironic best. *A Simple Story* (*Una storia semplice*) is, of course, infinitely more complicated than the teasing title implies. It opens with a telephone call to a police station at 7.30 on the evening of Saturday 18th March. 'The offices were almost deserted,' Sciascia observes, 'even more so than on other evenings at that hour, but they were still lit, the way the offices of the police were usually kept lit in the evening and during the night, by tacit agreement, to give the townspeople the impression that the police were ever alert to the safety of the public.' That observation, quietly sarcastic, establishes the tone of the narrative. Halfway through the story, a magistrate is questioning the elderly man who taught him many years earlier:

'Do you mind if I ask you a question?... I'll ask you another one after that, a very different one... You always gave me three for my Italian compositions, because I copied. But once you gave me five. Why?'

'Because you copied from a better writer.'

The magistrate burst out laughing. 'Italian! I was quite weak at Italian. But as you see, it hasn't been too much of a hindrance, here I am, a public prosecutor...'

'Italian isn't about Italian, it's about learning to think,' said the teacher. 'With less Italian, you might have risen even higher.'

It was nasty crack. The magistrate turned pale. And proceeded with a harsh interrogation.

This is Sciascia slyly commenting on the misuse of language, which was one of his favourite bugbears. Words employed thoughtlessly by those in positions of power is a constant theme in everything he wrote, whether criticism or fiction. The teacher is an intelligent and cultivated man, but he has reached that stage in life when he can only talk about his ills to the young police sergeant, who is by far the most attractive character in this cautionary tale. The sergeant learns from the teacher that 'hope isn't the last thing to die, but dying is the last hope.'

Sciascia was, in fact, a dying man when he wrote *A Simple Story*, the plot of which cannot be revealed because the revelation would spoil the pleasure of the readers coming fresh to it. The surprises keep on coming right up to the final paragraph. It's a masterly exercise in storytelling by an author who admired and learned from his great Sicilian predecessors Giovanni Verga and Pirandello.

Candido, a decidedly more skittish piece, dates from the 1970s. This 'dream dreamed in Sicily' is a retelling of Voltaire's satire on man's impossible search for Utopia, and it follows the adventures, if such they can be called, of Candido, who is born in a cave during a bombing raid on Sicily in 1943. His father is one of several discreditable lawyers in Sciascia's novels while his mother would rather be in the arms of an American soldier. His maternal grandfather is General Arturo Cressi of the Fascist militia, 'hero of the wars in Ethiopia and Spain and slightly less of a hero, thanks to the rheumatism from which he suffered, of the war currently in progress'. Candido has a loveless childhood and youth, thanks in part – as his name suggests – to his habit of telling the truth. The only affection he receives is from Concetta, the devout Catholic housekeeper who tends to see the worst in everybody. Sciascia has any number of targets in this short fantasy – the legal system, the church, the Christian Democrats who were in and out of office in the 1940s, '50s and

'60s. Candido is befriended in adolescence by an archpriest who is interested, to the point of obsession, in psychoanalysis. This is a topsy-turvy world, but a recognisable one nevertheless.

For reasons I find inexplicable, Leonardo Sciascia is virtually unknown in Britain. Perhaps it's because his crime novels are too close to reality. His murderers walk away free of the charges that ought to be their due. There's one such in *A Simple Story*. He's a disconcerting writer who is determined to make his readers think, as Orwell does. This book is a good place to discover him.

– Paul Bailey, 2010

Introduction

Leonardo Sciascia was above all else a Sicilian: that is the first and most significant thing to say about him. Born in the village of Racalmuto, near Agrigento (in the same region as Pirandello, another great Sicilian writer much obsessed with the meaning of truth, who is actually mentioned in *A Simple Story*), Sciascia spent almost his entire life on the island, and it is the setting for most of his work.

Yet he is an unusual kind of regional writer, one who does not celebrate his patch of earth as much as excoriate its failings. We find precious little local colour in Sciascia's work: no lyrical descriptions of landscape, no atmospheric evocations of heat and sunlight and sirocco, no loving details of indigenous customs. Sciascia is generally far less concerned with the surface of Sicilian life than with what goes on beneath the surface, the complex patterns of patronage and protection that underlie the island's society and politics, and, above all, the pervasive influence of the Mafia. Sicily quickly becomes, in his works, an almost abstract backdrop to an obsessive examination of the themes of justice – or rather, injustice – corruption and power, and the intricate nexus of connections between them.

For much of his life, Sciascia worked as a schoolteacher, and his literary work includes, apart from novels, a great many essays on political and social questions, as well as some powerful pieces of investigative journalism. (He also, as we shall see, actively participated in politics.) The polemical impulse is never very far away, even in his fiction, nor is the latter devoid of a certain didacticism, which often comes out in little authorial asides and comments. His tone is typically detached, ironic, distanced, and his stories are less about the psychology of his characters than the way those characters interact with one another and with the wider forces influencing their society. He was, in many ways, the model of a committed writer, who consciously used his work to analyse the problems he saw around him and contribute, in however small a way, to changing them.

In *A Simple Story*, Sciascia's last published work of fiction (by a strange twist of fate, it first appeared in bookshops on the very day that he died, November 20th 1989), he returns to a framework he often used in his career: the oblique detective story, in which a police investigation of a crime does not necessarily lead to a full revelation of the truth or to the punishment of the perpetrators. Having been among the first writers (if not the first), in his great novels of the Sixties, *The Day of the Owl* and *To Each His Own*, to talk explicitly about the Sicilian Mafia, not as an isolated criminal phenomenon, but as a political force pervading the island's power structures, Sciascia takes care never even to mention the word 'Mafia' in *A Simple Story*. He deliberately leaves vague the details of the criminal activities uncovered in the course of the story (although the reader may well have a pretty good idea by the end as to what they are) and the numbers of those involved in them. And even though two figures of authority have been implicated in the crimes by the end of the story (one of them apparently 'getting away with it'), Sciascia leaves open quite how far the web of corruption and collusion goes. Are the authorities merely incompetent, or do they know more than they are letting on? We never find out. The 'simple story' is revealed, of course, to be far from simple in its ramifications, and this little anecdote of an apparently minor series of incidents in a small Sicilian town can easily be seen (especially if the reader is familiar with other works by Sciascia covering similar ground) as symbolic of an all-pervading corruption in Sicilian society.

Candido, published in 1977, is on the face of it a very different proposition. It dates from what was certainly the most political period of Sciascia's career. Two years earlier, in 1975, he had agreed to stand as an independent candidate on the Communist ticket at the municipal elections in Palermo. Elected as a councillor, he was so disgusted by the behaviour of the Communist Party – at a time when they were involved in what was known as the 'historic compromise' with their old rivals, the Christian Democrats, and against a background of growing terrorist activity from both the Right and the Left – that he resigned at the beginning of 1977. Not long afterwards, he was elected as a deputy to the National Assembly, representing the Radical Party, and later became a member of the European Parliament.

Candido arose directly out of its author's experiences as a councillor between 1975 and 1977, as he himself readily acknowledged in a 1987 interview: 'I was never a Communist, and yet, to be honest, I must admit that I was attracted by the PCI [Italian Communist Party]. When I saw and realised, in the municipal council of Palermo, that this party, supposedly one of opposition, did not in any way play its role as an opposition, I stopped going along with it, and felt a sense of liberation. [...] I then wrote a parody of Voltaire's *Candide*, a parody that amused me and gave me an intense feeling of freedom. I always feel pleasure in writing; with *Candido*, this pleasure was even greater, because it gave me a chance to play, in a detached, light-hearted way, with quotations, references and allusions.'

It would be a mistake, I think, to read too much into *Candido*'s parallels with the Voltaire original. What Sciascia takes from *Candide* is the basic framework of an innocent abroad in a world full of perils and disasters, who discovers that the ideology propounded by his mentor – Leibnizian optimism as championed by Pangloss in *Candide*, Communism as upheld by Don Antonio in *Candido* – is inadequate to deal with those perils and disasters.

Adopting a dry, acerbic, Olympian manner in keeping with the eighteenth-century inspiration (in many ways merely an extension of his usual ironic, detached style), Sciascia uses this 'parody' of Voltaire not only to settle his accounts with the Communists and their compromises and contradictions, but also to take sideswipes at the Catholic Church, psychoanalysis, the vestiges of Fascism in post-war society, small-town hypocrisy, and (once again) the networks of patronage and collusion that stymie progress in Sicily. While the present-day non-Italian reader may find some of the topical references, ideological debates and literary allusions a touch abstruse, *Candido* remains of interest for its consistent humour and for the glimpses it gives us – and here it rejoins the main lines of Sciascia's work, as exemplified in *A Simple Story* – of a society ossified by corruption, cronyism and criminality. It is no surprise that Candido only finds happiness when he has left Sicily.

'In Sicily [...] nothing ever ends,' says Don Antonio at the end of *Candido*. Here, as in *A Simple Story*, Sciascia remains true to himself: a regional writer who, far from celebrating the uniqueness of his society, spent his career decrying the forces that have prevented it from changing.

– *Howard Curtis, 2010*

A Simple Story

Once again I want to carefully examine what
possibilities for justice still remain.
DÜRRENMATT, *The Execution of Justice*

The telephone call came in at 7.30 on the evening of March 18th, a Saturday, the eve of the noisy, colourful festival that the town held in honour of Saint Joseph the carpenter – and it was indeed the carpenter who seemed to have inspired the bonfires of old furniture which were lit in the working-class neighbourhoods almost as a promise to the few carpenters still in business that there would be no lack of work for them. The offices were almost deserted, even more so than on other evenings at that hour, but they were still lit, the way the offices of the police were usually kept lit in the evening and during the night, by tacit agreement, to give the townspeople the impression that the police were ever alert to the safety of the public.

The switchboard operator noted down the time and the caller's name: Giorgio Roccella. He was well-spoken, the voice calm and soft. 'Like all madmen,' the switchboard operator thought. This Signor Roccella asked to speak to the commissioner, which really was mad, especially at that hour and on that particular evening.

The switchboard operator made an effort to adopt the same tone, but succeeded only in sounding like a caricatured imitation, especially when he joked, 'A police commissioner at police headquarters? Not at this hour' – a quip that had done the rounds of the building, in reference to the commissioner's frequent absences. Then he added, 'I'll put you through to the superintendent,' thinking to play a trick on the superintendent, who was probably on the point of leaving his office at that moment.

The superintendent was, in fact, just putting on his coat. It was the sergeant, whose desk was at an angle to the superintendent's, who took the call. He listened, looked for a pencil and a piece of paper on the desk, and, as he wrote, replied that yes, they would go as soon as they could, absolutely as soon as they could, thus planting the possibility that there might be some delay and expectations should not be raised.

'Who was it?' the superintendent asked.

'A man who says he's found something in his house and wants to show it to us urgently.'

'A body?' the superintendent joked.

'No, he said it was a thing.'

'A thing... And what's this man's name?'

The sergeant took the sheet of paper on which he had written the name and address and read, 'Giorgio Roccella, Cotugno district, four kilometres from the Monterosso fork, along the right-hand road, fifteen from here.'

The superintendent walked back from the door to the sergeant's table, picked up the paper and read it, almost as though he thought he might find on it something more than the sergeant had already told him. 'It's not possible,' he said.

'What isn't?' the sergeant asked.

'This Roccella,' the superintendent said, 'is a diplomat, a consul or ambassador somewhere or other. He hasn't lived here for years, his house in town is all shut up, and the one in the country, in Cotugno in fact, is abandoned and almost in ruins. You can see it from the road. Up on top there, looks like a blockhouse.'

'An old farmhouse,' the sergeant said. 'I've passed it many times.'

'It's because there's a perimeter wall around it, that's what makes it look like a farm. But there's a really pretty house – or at least there was... A big family, the Roccellas, but now the only one left is this consul or ambassador, or whatever he is... I didn't even know he was still alive, he's been gone so long.'

'If you like,' the sergeant said, 'I can go over there and check it out.'

'No, no, I'm sure it's a hoax… Maybe you can take a look tomorrow, if you have the time and the inclination… As for me, whatever happens, don't try to get hold of me. I'm celebrating Saint Joseph's at a friend of mine's, out in the country.'

2

The next day, the sergeant went out to Cotugno district in the patrol car. He and the two officers with him were in the mood for an excursion: from what the superintendent had said, they were sure the place was uninhabited and that the call the previous evening had been a hoax. There was nothing left of the stream that had flowed at the foot of the hill except a dried-up bed filled with stones as white as bones, but the hill itself, with that ruined farmhouse at the top, was turning green. Once they had inspected the place, they planned to have a jolly time gathering asparagus and chicory: all three men were of peasant stock and were good at recognising decent wild vegetables.

They entered the perimeter, which did not consist simply of walls, as might be supposed from the outside: there were a number of storerooms, with shiny bolts on the doors, surrounding the house, which was indeed pretty, although clearly decaying. They walked around it. All the windows had shutters on them, except for one that you could see through. As the light on that March morning was glaring, they could not see much inside at first. Then they started to make out something and all three, shielding their eyes from the sun with their hands, tried again, sure now that they could see a man sitting with his back to the window, his head resting on a desk.

The sergeant took the decision to break the pane of glass, open the window and go in: the man might have been taken ill, and they might still be in time to help him. But the man was dead – and not from a heart attack or anything like that: there was a blackish clot on his head between the lower jaw and the temple.

To the two officers, who had also climbed in through the window, the sergeant cried, 'Don't touch a thing!' Rather than touch the telephone on the desk, he ordered one of the officers to drive to headquarters, report what had happened, and come straight back with a doctor, a photographer and the two or three people at headquarters who were supposed to be forensics experts – only supposed to be, according to the sergeant, who couldn't recall a single case to date on which their findings had been decisive, rather than just muddying the waters.

Having given his orders, and again telling the officer who had stayed with him not to touch a thing, the sergeant started to have a look around, thinking of the written report he would have to make later: always a thankless task, as his years of schooling and the few books he had read had not sufficed to give him confidence in the Italian language. But, curiously, having to write down the things he saw and the anxiety this caused him sharpened his abilities to select, to pare down, to express things pithily, so that only what was sound and perceptive remained in the net of his writing. Such may be the case with Italian writers from the south, especially Sicilians – in spite of school, university and lots of reading.

His first impression was that the man had committed suicide. The gun was on the floor, to the right of the armchair on which he had been sitting: an old German weapon from the First World War, the kind of gun soldiers brought back with them from the front as a souvenir. But there was one detail that contradicted the sergeant's impression of suicide: the dead man's right hand, which should have been dangling directly above the fallen pistol, was actually on the desk, on top of a sheet of paper containing the words: *I've found.* That full stop after the word *found* was like a flashbulb going off inside the sergeant's mind, conjuring up, however briefly, a murder scene to replace the hastily constructed suicide scenario. The man had started to write *I've found–* just as, when phoning headquarters, he had said he'd found something he hadn't expected to find. Starting to have his doubts that the police would ever come, perhaps also starting, in the solitude and the silence, to feel afraid, he had been about to write down what he had found when he had heard a knock at the door. 'The police,' he thought: instead of which, it was the killer. Perhaps he pretended to be a policeman, and the man let him in and started to tell him about what he had found. Perhaps the pistol was on the desk: most likely, feeling increasingly scared, he had gone and got it out of some boxroom he remembered (the sergeant did not believe that killers would go armed with such old weapons). Seeing it on the desk, the killer may have asked him about the weapon, may have checked how it worked, and suddenly aimed it at the man's head and fired. And then he'd had that great idea of putting the full stop after *I've found*: *I've found that life isn't worth living, I've found the one truth, the ultimate truth, I've found, I've found*: everything and nothing. No, it didn't really add up. But assuming it was true, then the full stop wasn't a mistake on the killer's part: if the suicide theory was brought up (and the sergeant was sure it would be), all sorts of existential and philosophical meanings would be derived from that full stop, especially if there was anything in the dead man's personality to support them. There was a bunch of keys on the desk, along with an old pewter inkpot and a photograph of a large, happy group, taken in the garden at least fifty years earlier: just outside here, perhaps, when there were probably trees round the house, bringing harmony and shade, where now there were only withered branches and scrub.

Next to the sheet of paper with the words *I've found* was a fountain pen with the top on: a neat touch on the part of the killer (the sergeant was ever more certain that it had been murder), giving the impression that with that full stop the man had indeed put a clear full stop to his own existence.

The bookshelves around the room were almost entirely empty. The few books that remained were bound yearly volumes of legal journals, manuals of agronomy, issues of a magazine called *Nature and Art*. There was also a pile of very old-looking volumes, on the backs of which the sergeant read the word *Calepinus*. The word suggested to him a small book you kept in your pocket, a little notebook: odd to use that name for these books, each of which weighed at least ten kilos. His concern not to leave fingerprints, even though he didn't believe in them, took away any curiosity he might have felt to open one of these volumes, and because of the same concern, he wandered through the house, followed by the officer, without touching furniture or door handles, only entering rooms whose doors were open.

The house was much larger than it looked from the outside. There was a big dining room with a solid oak table and four sideboards of the same wood. Inside them, plates, soup dishes, cups and coffee pots, as well as old toys, papers, linen. Three bedrooms, two with mattresses and cushions piled up on the bases of the beds, the third one with a bed that looked as if it had been slept in the night before. There might have been other bedrooms behind the doors the sergeant didn't open. The house had been abandoned and even stripped of fittings, books, pictures and china (some of the missing things had left marks) but did not give the impression that it had been unoccupied. There were cigarette ends in the ashtrays, and dregs of wine in five glasses that had been taken into the kitchen with the clear intention of washing them. The kitchen was spacious, with wood fireplaces, an oven, Valencian tiles. Copper pots and pans hung on the walls, gleaming slightly in the dim light, even though they were turning green with sulphate. From the kitchen, a little door led to a narrow staircase, so dark that you couldn't see where it ended.

The sergeant tried to find a light switch so that he could see his way upstairs. All he found was the one that lit the lights over the fireplaces, but he started up the stairs anyway. After five or six steps, still climbing hesitantly, he started lighting matches. He had to light a lot of them before he got to the top, where there was a kind of attic. The ceiling was so low that someone of normal height could almost touch it with his head, but the room covered as large an area as the dining room downstairs. It was full of sagging sofas, armchairs and chairs, crates, empty picture frames and dusty drapery. All around were busts of saints, ten of them gilded, and a larger one that stood out from the rest, with a silver chest, a black hood, and a cross-looking face. Each of the gilded busts carried the name of the saint on its baroque base, apart from the larger, darker one: the sergeant didn't know enough about saints to recognise it as Saint Ignatius.

The sergeant lit the last match and hurried back downstairs. 'An attic full of saints,' he said to the other officer, who was waiting for him at the foot of the stairs. He felt as though he had been showered with dust, cobwebs and mildew. He climbed out through the window, back to the cold but glorious morning, the sun, the grass dripping with hoarfrost.

He walked around the house, the officer following a couple of paces behind. Between the scrub and the withered branches, there was an open space, where cars, perhaps lorries, had clearly manoeuvred. 'There's been traffic here,' the sergeant said. Then he pointed to the bolts on the doors of the stable-like storerooms that surrounded the house like a fort in a Western and asked the officer, 'What do you think of those?'

'They're new,' the officer said.

'Congratulations,' the sergeant said.

3

Within less than two hours, all the people who were supposed to be there were there: the police commissioner, the public prosecutor, a doctor, a photographer, a journalist favoured by the commissioner, and a whole swarm of officers, among whom the forensics people stood out for their air of self-importance. There were six or seven cars which, even after they had arrived, continued to roar, screech and snarl, just as they had when they had left the centre of town, arousing the curiosity of the citizens and even of the Carabinieri: something the commissioner would have preferred to delay as long as possible. That was why the colonel from the Carabinieri, grim-faced, very angry, ready for a quarrel – with all due respect – with the commissioner, arrived half an hour later, by which time all the doors had already been opened with the keys found on the desk, fingerprints had been lifted, somewhat haphazardly, and the dead man photographed from all sides.

'You could have informed us,' the colonel said, with contained fury.

'I'm sorry,' the commissioner said, 'but it all happened so quickly, we only had a few minutes.'

'Yes, yes...' the colonel said ironically.

The gun was lifted by putting a pencil through the trigger loop, and then gently set down on a black cloth and carefully wrapped. 'Get prints right away,' the commissioner said. The dead man's prints had already been taken. 'Pointless, really,' he opined, 'but it has to be done.'

'Why pointless?' the colonel asked.

'Suicide,' the commissioner said gravely, thereby determining that the colonel would start to take the opposite view.

'Commissioner –' the sergeant butted in.

'Whatever you have to say, you can say in your report... In

the meantime…' But he had no idea what to say or do in the meantime, except repeat, 'Suicide, a clear case of suicide.'

The sergeant tried again. 'Commissioner –' He wanted to tell him about last night's phone call, and about that full stop after *I've found*. But the commissioner cut him off again. 'We need the report' – he indicated himself and the public prosecutor, and looked at his watch – 'first thing in the afternoon.' Then, to the prosecutor and the colonel, 'This is a simple case, we don't want to blow it all out of proportion, we just need to deal with it as quickly as possible… Go and write your report, right now.'

Automatically, the colonel saw this, rather, as a very complicated case, and certainly not one that could be dealt with as quickly as possible. So it was that, before anything had happened, a total disparity was established in the points of view of the institutions these two representatives embodied: the Carabinieri and the police. A long-standing historical feud divided them, and any citizen who got caught in the middle was left tragically floundering.

'Yes, sir,' the sergeant said, and went out to look for the patrol car he had come in, which had returned from town. But as the commissioner's attitude had annoyed him, and as he was almost entirely devoid of what is usually called *esprit de corps* – which meant regarding the body to which he belonged as the most important thing of all, considering it infallible, or, if it was fallible, untouchable, overwhelmingly right, especially when it was wrong – he had a mischievous idea.

A driver was sitting at the wheel of the car which had brought the colonel: a sergeant in the Carabinieri. Our sergeant went and sat down next to him – he knew him well, although they weren't friends – and told him everything he knew about the case, all his suspicions. He even pointed out those shiny new bolts on the doors of the storerooms. He felt lighter on his way back to the office, where he took more than two hours to write down what he had told his counterpart in five minutes.

So it was that, by the time he got back to town, the Carabinieri colonel had heard from his sergeant everything he needed to make the case more complicated than the commissioner desired.

4

Even though it was a Sunday, and the feast of Saint Joseph, personal details, details of ownership and a certain amount of fairly confidential information immediately flooded in to police headquarters and the Carabinieri's barracks. More or less the same information, from the same sources, the same informants: if they had cooperated, one of the two sides would have been spared a lot of time and effort which they could have used more profitably. But that would be to envisage something as impossible as a builder and a demolition expert cooperating (not that either of the sides could have been attributed such roles).

The identity of the victim: Giorgio Roccella, a retired diplomat, born in Monterosso on January 14th 1923. He had been Italian consul in various cities in Europe, and had finally settled in Edinburgh where, separated from his wife, he lived with his son, who was twenty. He had not been back to Italy in about fifteen years, coming back only to meet his tragic death on March 18th 1989. He had been the only one in his family to retain some of the extensive and varied property that had belonged to them – a half-ruined house in town, and that house in the country surrounded by a little bit of land – although he had done nothing to maintain them. He had arrived in town that very day, the 18th, had had lunch at a restaurant called *Le Tre Candele*, ordering spaghetti in sepia and octopus in a salad, and had then taken a taxi to his house in the country. There, he had asked the taxi driver to wait while he checked that the keys he had still opened the front door, after which he dismissed him, asking him to pick him up the next day at eleven in the morning. 'I suffer from insomnia,' he had said, 'I'm going to work all night.' But the next day at eleven, seeing the police and the Carabinieri bustling about, the taxi driver had turned back without going up to the house. Perhaps the man was a dangerous fugitive, he thought. Why go looking for trouble?

The commissioner, fairly rattled by the sergeant's report, which hinted at murder, saw in the fact that the victim had separated from his wife (or rather, that his wife had separated from him) evidence to support his suicide theory. The question as to why he should first have called the police was one that did occur to him, but without troubling him unduly. The man, he told himself, had decided to commit suicide with the police watching, to make his gesture more original, more sensational. In a word, he'd gone mad. But the sergeant, who had read the transcript of the information more attentively, pointed out to the commissioner that the separation had occurred twelve years earlier. However painful it may have been, it was unlikely to have driven him to a pitch of despair twelve years later. What did reach a pitch was the commissioner's irritation with the sergeant. 'Stop saying these things,' he said. 'And get the super-intendent back here immediately, wherever he is.'

5

As he had announced on Saturday, the superintendent was incommunicado until Monday morning. He arrived at the office at eight o'clock, after the sergeant, wearing his hat and coat, his mouth covered with a scarf, and with his gloves on. He shivered as he took everything off. 'It's almost as cold in here as it is outside: even the birds would drop down dead in here.'

He had heard what had happened from the radio and the newspapers, he said. He read the sergeant's sketchy report without comment and went out to confer with the commissioner.

When he came back, he seemed to have it in for the sergeant. 'Let's not go inventing stories,' he warned him. But the stories were already in the air. Two hours later, Carmelo Franzò, a teacher and an old friend of the victim's, was sitting in the office adding to them. The way he told it was that on Saturday the 18th, he had received an unexpected visit from Giorgio Roccella. The reason for this sudden journey: he had remembered two bundles of old letters in a chest that was probably still in the attic of his house in the country – one of letters to his great-grandfather from Garibaldi and the other of letters to his grandfather from Pirandello (they had been at school together) – and the idea had occurred to him to find them and do a bit of work on them. He asked his friend if he would go with him to the house that afternoon, but it was the very afternoon the teacher was due his regular dialysis, which he couldn't get out of unless he wanted to be in a poisoned, immobile state for days. He really would have liked to go back to the house after all these years and take part in the search. They arranged to meet the next day, Sunday, but on Sunday evening he heard the news of his friend's death on the radio.

But the teacher had something else to tell them, something important. On Saturday evening, he had had a phone call from his friend. He was phoning from the house, and the first thing he said was, 'I didn't know they'd installed a phone here.' Then he told him that while looking for the letters in the attic, he had found, guess what, the famous painting. 'What painting?' the teacher had asked. 'The one that disappeared a few years ago, don't you remember?' Roccella had said. The teacher had no idea what painting he was talking about, but advised him to call the police.

'What a complicated story,' the superintendent said, torn between incredulity and anxiety. 'The painting, the telephone… both of them only just discovered by Signor Roccella when he spoke to you…' Ever more incredulous, he asked the teacher, 'Did you believe him?'

'I've believed him all my life, why should I have stopped believing him the other night?'

Meanwhile, the sergeant had picked up the phone book and leafed through it. 'Roccella, Giorgio,' he read, 'Monterosso, Cotugno district, 342260… It's in the book.'

'Thank you,' the superintendent said sourly. 'But that's not what interests me. What I find intriguing is that he didn't know anything about it.'

'We could – ' the sergeant began.

'You could, and you will, immediately… Go to the telephone company and get all the details: how the application was made, the date the phone was installed, when the bills were paid… Get photocopies of everything…' He turned back to the teacher. 'Let's talk about the famous painting: first it disappeared, then your friend found it, and now apparently it's disappeared again… I get the feeling you have an idea what painting your friend was referring to…'

'What about you?' the teacher replied.

'Not me,' the superintendent said. 'I don't know anything about paintings. I do know there are a lot of missing ones in

Italy, and I have a friend who's an expert on them. We'll consult him... But in the meantime, tell me about this missing painting. What, in your opinion – '

'I'm no expert on missing paintings,' the teacher said.

'But you must have an opinion.'

'No different from yours, I should think.'

'Christ, it's always the same... Even with teachers.'

'Even with superintendents,' the teacher retorted sharply.

The superintendent restrained himself: if it had been anyone else, he might have thrown him in the holding cells. But Signor Franzò was known and respected all over town, generations of pupils remembered him with affection and gratitude. So, instead, he said, 'Please repeat to me as accurately as possible what your friend said to you in person and over the phone.'

Nervously, he set about repeating his story, so nervously that he spelt it out slowly, step by step.

'Are you sure you're not leaving anything out?' the superintendent asked, by way of revenge.

'I have a good memory and I'm not in the habit of leaving anything out.'

'All right,' the superintendent said, 'but remember: you'll soon have to repeat everything word for word to the judge.'

The teacher gave a half-indulgent, half-disdainful smile. But the skirmish was interrupted by the entrance of the commissioner, who had been a pupil of the teacher.

'You here?'

'And with an interesting story to tell,' the superintendent said.

Just then the sergeant returned, with a new upset. 'The application was made three years ago, but using a false signature... The Carabinieri have already established that.'

'Damn!' the commissioner cried – a curse directed at the Carabinieri.

6

But now that, thanks to the teacher's testimony, the suicide theory, which the commissioner had been the first to accept and the colonel of the Carabinieri had immediately rejected, had faded away, they were both urged by their superiors to meet and exchange information, theories and suspicions. Which they did, through clenched teeth, so to speak, although they couldn't quite manage to be totally vague and unreasonable.

This was their reconstruction: Signor Roccella, having got the idea into his head of finding the letters from Garibaldi and Pirandello, had returned unexpectedly after many years away; had gone to see his old friend; had had lunch in a restaurant; had picked up the keys to the country house from his house in town, unless he already had them with him; had been driven there in a taxi. Once there, having made sure the keys still fitted the locks, he had been left alone to carry out his search. But what had happened after that? He had discovered that a phone had been installed, but, from what the teacher had said, hadn't seemed all that surprised. Which meant that he had some idea who had had it installed. What, however, had surprised him, and perhaps scared him, was discovering that painting in the attic where he had gone to look for the letters. He had phoned his friend, and then the police. And as the police were taking their time coming, he had started writing *I've found...* Really scared by now, he had gone and fished out the old Mauser. It was most likely at that moment that he had heard a knock at the door. The police, at last. He had gone to open – but it was his killer.

Several points needed to be checked. Had the phone really been installed without his being aware of it? Was his desire to find those letters by Garibaldi and Pirandello the real reason for his return? Had he really found that missing painting, or was it an old family painting he'd forgotten about, which had turned up among all the clutter in the attic?

They would have to search the house again, more thoroughly this time. But while they were making their minds up about that, something else happened, something that was to cost them a great deal of work and disruption.

A local train, which, as usual at that hour – two in the afternoon – was full of students, had been halted by the signals before the station at Monterosso. It had waited for the signal to change, but half an hour had gone by and the signal remained red.

The main road ran parallel to the railway line. Students and railwaymen swarmed onto it, cursing the stationmaster at Monterosso, who had either forgotten to give the go signal or had fallen asleep.

There were not many cars on the road at that hour and only one driver stopped to ask what had happened to the train. The car was a Volvo, and the guard asked the driver to do him a favour: to go to the station at Monterosso and wake up the stationmaster. The Volvo drove up to the station, stopped, then disappeared. It must have come back down along another road.

After a while, as the signal was still red, the guard, followed by a few passengers, walked the five hundred metres to the station. There, they were horrified to discover that the stationmaster and the engineer were indeed asleep, and would remain so forever. They had been killed.

The police and the Carabinieri were both called, and they immediately set off in search of the Volvo driver. He wouldn't be difficult to find, as there were no more than thirty Volvos in the whole of the province. The Volvo driver must have thought the same thing when he heard on the radio that the police were looking for him and realised they'd find him sooner rather than later. So he went to police headquarters, reluctantly and with trepidation but, as was written at the beginning of his statement, of his own free will.

Name and surname, date and place of birth, address, profession, had he ever had any dealings with the law?

'Not even a parking ticket,' the man said. But his stated profession – pharmaceuticals salesman – gave the superintendent the unutterable joy of launching into the interrogation on a harsh note.

'So you own a Volvo?'

'Obviously.'

'Don't say "obviously" when you're speaking to me... A Volvo's quite an expensive car.'

The man nodded.

'Do the drugs you sell include cocaine, heroin and opium?'

'Listen,' the man said, holding back his anger and fear, 'I came here of my own free will, to tell you what I saw yesterday afternoon.'

'So tell us,' the superintendent said, with an incredulous air.

'I drove up to the station, just as the guard asked me to. I knocked at the window of the stationmaster's office, and he opened – '

'Who?'

'The stationmaster, I think.'

'So you didn't know him?'

'No. I told him what the guard had told me to tell him. I glanced inside the office. There were two other men there, rolling up a carpet... Then I drove away.'

'By a different road,' the superintendent said. 'No one saw you coming back down... So – they were rolling up a carpet.'

'The painting,' the sergeant blurted out.

The superintendent glared at him. 'Thank you, but I'd have got there without your help.'

'Oh, no,' the sergeant said, 'I wouldn't dare to...' And in his confusion, he stammered, naively, 'You're a graduate.'

The words sounded ironic to the superintendent, and made him lose his temper completely – but with the Volvo driver. 'I'm sorry, but we have to keep you here: we need to check out your story.'

Sergeant Antonio Lagandara had been born in a village so close to the town that it could now be considered part of it. His father, a day labourer who had managed to raise himself and become an expert pruner, much in demand, had died, overbalancing while stripping a tall cherry tree of withered branches, when Antonio was in the last year of an economics and business studies course. He had obtained his diploma but, unsure what to do next, had joined the police, and within five years had become a sergeant. He loved the job, and wanted to make his way to the top. He had enrolled in the law faculty, attended it as and when he could, and studied. Graduating in law was his greatest ambition, his dream, so the words which had sounded malicious to the superintendent were in fact perfectly innocent. The superintendent was still feeling offended when the sergeant came back from the holding cells, where he had left the Volvo driver protesting so loudly that his howls could be heard all over the building. 'So, I'm a graduate, eh? I still can't figure out whether you're really naive or just pretending... A graduate! Everyone's a graduate these days: ushers, waiters, even road sweepers.'

'I'm sorry,' the sergeant said, sincerely but in a surly tone.

'Forget it... I'm going to see the commissioner now: in a quarter of an hour bring the Volvo driver to his office.'

The colonel from the Carabinieri was in the commissioner's office, and the superintendent brought them both up to date. When the sergeant brought in the Volvo driver, the commissioner said immediately, 'So you saw two men rolling up a carpet in the stationmaster's office. Was there a corpse in it?'

'A corpse? Certainly not.'

'How wide was the carpet?'

'I don't know... Maybe a metre and a half.'

'How can you be sure it was a carpet?' the colonel asked.

'I'm not sure of anything: I just thought it was a carpet.'

'Describe it.'

'It looked to me as if they were rolling it up back to front. The surface was rough, like canvas…'

'But that's not what the back of a carpet looks like. Is it possible they were actually rolling up a painting?'

'It's possible,' the man said.

'Let's talk about something else… You say there were three men?'

'That's right, three.'

The commissioner showed him two photographs. 'Do you recognise these two?'

They were trying to set a trap for him: he cursed them inwardly. 'What do you mean? I don't think I've ever seen these two in my life.'

'You know who they are? The stationmaster and the engineer: the men who were murdered.'

'But I've never seen them!'

'You said you saw the stationmaster, and even spoke to him!'

'I spoke to someone I thought was the stationmaster.'

'I'm sorry,' the commissioner said, 'but I'm obliged to keep you here a while longer.'

The unfortunate man again howled in protest.

The commissioner and the colonel brought the examining magistrate up to date with the investigation. The magistrate assumed a grave, thoughtful air and then said, 'You know what I think? It may well have been by chance, but I think the Volvo driver went inside the stationmaster's office, saw the painting, grabbed it, killed the two men, and took it away with him.'

The commissioner and the colonel exchanged baffled, ironic glances.

'I felt there was something about that Volvo driver straight away. My intuition's not usually wrong. Keep him behind bars.' He dismissed them, because he had to question Signor Franzò the teacher.

On the way out, the commissioner said, 'My God!' and the colonel, 'Unbelievable!'

Meanwhile, the magistrate had risen to greet his old teacher. 'How wonderful to see you again after all these years!'

'A lot of years,' the teacher agreed, 'and I feel every one of them.'

'What do you mean? You haven't changed a bit.'

'You have,' the teacher said, with his usual honesty.

'This damned job... But you do remember me?'

'Of course I remember you.'

'Do you mind if I ask you a question?... I'll ask you another one after that, a very different one... You always gave me three for my Italian compositions, because I copied. But once you gave me a five. Why?'

'Because you copied from a better writer.'

The magistrate burst out laughing. 'Italian! I was quite weak at Italian. But as you see, it hasn't been too much of a hindrance, here I am, a public prosecutor...'

'Italian isn't about Italian, it's about learning to think,' said the teacher. 'With less Italian, you might have risen even higher.'

It was a nasty crack. The magistrate turned pale. And proceeded with a harsh interrogation.

9

The victim's son and wife arrived the same day, the son from Edinburgh, the wife from Stuttgart. It was not a pleasant encounter, either for the two of them or for the investigators present. The wife had clearly come to grab as much as she could of the inheritance, and her son to stop her doing so, but above all to know how and why his father had been murdered, and by whom.

The encounter took place in the commissioner's office. They acknowledged each other's presence, the son's greeting being a curt 'You can go back to Stuttgart, there's nothing for you here.'

'According to you.'

'Not according to me, according to the papers my father had registered some years ago.'

'I'm not sure those papers are worth anything, or that they can't be contested… Let's come to an agreement: we sell everything and go.'

'I'm not selling: I may stay here. I came here many years ago and stayed for quite a while, when my grandparents were still alive. I have very pleasant memories of the place… Yes, I may stay. My father and I often talked about coming back and settling here.'

'Your father!' the woman said sarcastically.

'You mean he wasn't my father? Listen: we don't choose our mothers, or I certainly wouldn't have chosen you… And I'm sure you would never have chosen me as a son… But we can choose our fathers, and I chose Giorgio, I loved him, and I'm really sorry he's dead. He was my father. You're making far too much of the fact that you slept with another man, or other men.'

In a flash, his mother's hand, with its rings and its polished nails, struck his cheek. The young man turned his back on her and started looking at the bookcase as if the books really interested him. He was crying.

The commissioner said, 'All that's your business. What I want to hear from you, signora, is if you know of any reason why your husband was murdered, if you suspect anyone.'

The woman shrugged her shoulders. 'He was a Sicilian,' she said, 'and for some reason Sicilians have been killing each other for years.'

'A judgement nobody could argue with,' the son said ironically, sitting down again in front of the commissioner's desk.

'What about you?' the commissioner asked him. 'Do you know anything?'

'About why he was killed? I have no idea. In fact I hope you'll be able to tell me eventually... Apart from that...' He told him what he knew: his father's decision to come back in order to find those letters from Garibaldi and Pirandello, his own regret that he had been unable to accompany him, the phone call he had received from his father assuring him that he had had a very good journey. That was all.

'Tell me something about your properties here. Were they really abandoned?'

'Yes and no. Every now and again he would write to someone, a priest I think, to find out what state they were in.'

'Was the priest responsible for their upkeep?'

'I don't think so, not really.'

'Did your father send him money?'

'Not as far as I know.'

'Did he answer your father's letters?'

'Yes, he always said everything was fine, even though the houses were empty.'

'Did this priest have keys to both houses?'

'I don't know.'

'Do you remember his name?'

'Cricco, I think... Father Cricco. But I'm not sure.'

Father Cricco – a handsome man, tall and solemn in his cassock – stated that he had never had the keys, all he ever did was take a look at both houses from the outside and make sure that they were still standing, with no visible cracks, no erosion that couldn't be repaired.

The superintendent asked the questions in a considerate, complimentary manner, while the sergeant took down the statement. 'You're one of the few priests who still dress as priests,' the superintendent began. 'I find that quite cheering, for some reason.'

'I'm a priest of the old school, and you're a Catholic of the old school. Good for us, if I say so myself.'

'As a priest, as an intelligent man, and as a friend of the dead man, what do you think of this case?'

'Despite all the stories that have been circulated, I must confess I can't get the idea of suicide out of my head. Giorgio was not a man at peace with himself.'

'Right: his wife, the son who wasn't his son…'

'But apparently the forensics people…'

'Yes, they found the dead man's prints on the gun, but in the places where he would have had to grip it to shoot himself, they seem to have been rubbed out, as if someone wearing gloves had held it… But with all due respect to the forensics people, I don't really trust their findings.'

The sergeant, who had not lost the habit of intervening, said, 'I don't trust them either, not at all. Imagine a man who's holding a gun and just about to kill himself, putting his glove on, firing and then having time to take his glove off again and get rid of it. The whole thing's absurd.'

'You're enjoying yourself, I see,' the superintendent said, sourly. 'Carry on enjoying yourself.'

The police and the legal authorities decided to do another search of the house, with Roccella's wife and son present, as well as Signor Franzò the teacher. The superintendent went, and the sergeant, and a swarm of officers. Father Cricco declined the invitation: it would have been too emotional for him, and there was no real point in his being there.

It was the sergeant who went to pick up the teacher from his house. They were alone together for the brief journey, much to the sergeant's delight: talking to people who had the reputation of being intelligent and cultured filled him with a kind of exhilaration. But the teacher talked about his own ills, and the only thing the sergeant took away from it all was the idea – not one he could share, as an energetic thirty-year-old – that when you get to a certain point in your life, hope isn't the last thing to die, but dying is the last hope.

The teacher knew the place well, he had spent many hours there with his friend during his childhood and adolescence. As soon as they entered the perimeter, he pointed to the storerooms and said, 'They used to be the stables.' But the sergeant was surprised to see the doors wide open, the bolts gone. It must have been the Carabinieri, he thought. He told the superintendent, and once they were inside the house they telephoned the Carabinieri. No, it hadn't been them, they didn't know anything about it.

Nervously, the sergeant inspected the storerooms one by one. They had an indefinable odour, a mixture of burnt sugar, crushed eucalyptus leaves, alcohol. 'Do you smell it?' he asked the superintendent.

'I can't smell anything, I have a bad cold.'

'We ought to bring an expert in, a chemist. The customs police can let us have some sniffer dogs.'

'You're the best sniffer dog we have,' the superintendent said. 'But all right, we will bring in the experts and the dogs.'

The others were waiting outside the front door of the house. The superintendent had the keys. 'Open it up,' he said, giving them to the sergeant. 'You can be our guide. It's the first time I've been here.'

They all swarmed inside, the police officers as wildly as if they hoped to surprise a burglar, the boy looking around, his eyes moist with emotion, the woman quite cool, as if bored.

On the ground floor, there was nothing the officers had not already seen. They climbed to the first floor, and entered the kitchen. The door leading up to the attic was mysteriously open. They stood there waiting, until the superintendent stepped forward and climbed the wooden staircase nimbly and confidently. Once he had got to the top, he flooded the attic with light. The others followed him up.

The sergeant, moving cautiously among the piles of junk, kept looking at the walls.

'What are you looking for?' the superintendent asked.

'The light switch.'

'Oh, yes, you never could find it. But it isn't hard: it's behind the bust of Saint Ignatius.'

'But you can't see it,' the sergeant said.

'I just sensed it,' the superintendent said. 'Don't tell me I found it because I'm a graduate,' he went on, making a joke of it. But his eyes had glazed over, as if in terror.

'I won't,' the sergeant said.

12

On the chest was an area not covered by the thick layer of dust that covered everything else, a clear sign that something had been left lying there quite a while. The rolled-up painting, the sergeant thought – and said so. Poor Roccella must have seen it even before he opened the chest and looked for the letters. The letters were there, in bundles: the ones from Garibaldi, and the ones from Pirandello. The teacher had actually seen them, many years before. He leafed through the letters by Pirandello, lingering over a few phrases. At eighteen, Pirandello had already been thinking the same things he would write about when he was over sixty.

On the journey back, the teacher said to the sergeant, 'I'd like to have a good look at those letters from Pirandello.'

'I don't think it would be difficult to arrange for you to have them.' But he was thinking of something else. He was sombre, uneasy, nervous: it was clear he needed to confide in someone, to get things off his chest. After a while he stopped the car and in his nervousness began to cry. 'We've been together for three years, in the same office.'

'I understand,' the teacher said. 'The light switch?'

'The light switch... He said he'd never set foot in the house before – you heard him, too... I used up a whole box of matches, looking for that light switch. The others used their torches to look for it... Yet he found it straight away, with no problem.'

'An incredible mistake on his part,' the teacher said.

'But how could he have made a mistake like that, what happened to him in that moment?'

'Perhaps he suddenly felt as though he was cut in two: in that moment he was both the criminal and the policeman chasing him.' And enigmatically, as if to himself, he added, 'Pirandello.'

'I want to tell you everything. Starting with the light switch, I've been adding it all up, like arithmetic.'

'Arithmetic…' The teacher smiled. 'But you're still not sure about a few things.'

'That's why I'm asking you to help me.'

'If I can… But come up to my place: we won't be disturbed there.'

They talked for hours, and reached the conclusion that, for the criminals, the painting had been an impulsive pleasure, a marginal activity, almost a whim. They had been doing something quite different in the house and that was why Roccella, arriving unexpectedly, had been murdered.

At the door, about to take his leave, the teacher asked, 'What do you intend to –?'

'I don't know,' the sergeant said, wearily, at a loss. 'I don't know.'

13

The next day, the superintendent got to the office at the usual time, flaunting his usual good humour, which was close to euphoria. He took off his hat, his gloves, his coat, his bright but elegant scarf, put the gloves in the coat pocket, and hung everything in the wardrobe. The gloves. While the superintendent shook with cold, saying as he did every morning that even the birds would drop down dead here, the sergeant, who was already at his own desk, was shaking, too, but in a different way. The gloves, there they were, the gloves.

'Hard at work already?' the superintendent said, by way of greeting.

'I'm not working, I'm looking at the newspapers.'

'Anything good?'

'Nothing good, as usual.'

Beneath this exchange of banal, everyday phrases, there was an unease, a coolness between them, a sense of anxiety and fear.

The light switch. The glove. The sergeant did not know – nor would he have appreciated – a famous series of etchings by Max Klinger actually called *A glove*, but in his mind the superintendent's glove whizzed about just as it once had in the imagination of Max Klinger.

Their desks were at right angles to each other. Each man sat behind his own desk, the superintendent pretending to be absorbed in reading the documents in front of him, the sergeant in reading the newspapers.

Several times, the sergeant was on the point of getting up, going to see the commissioner and telling him everything. What held him back was the thought that everything he had to say would seem quite flimsy to the commissioner. The superintendent – the sergeant realised suddenly – had had another, more immediately lethal idea.

At a certain point, the superintendent stood up, went to a little cupboard and took out a small bottle of lubricating oil, a woollen cloth, and a pipe-cleaner. 'I haven't cleaned this pistol in ages,' he said. He took it out of the holster on his belt and placed it on his desk. Then he opened it, and dropped the cartridges on the desk.

The sergeant understood. On the newspaper he had in front of him, which he was pretending to read, the words moved and merged together, dissolving into the headline the superintendent could imagine reading in the next day's papers: *Police superintendent accidentally kills one of his subordinates.*

He said, 'I always clean mine... But are you a good shot?'

'Excellent,' the superintendent said.

And the sergeant, by way of warning and to get it off his conscience, said, 'It's not enough to hit the centre of a target to be considered a good shot. It takes skill, speed...'

'I know.'

No, the sergeant thought, you don't know, or at least you don't know the way I know.

Every morning he put his pistol in the top right-hand drawer of his desk. Now he opened the drawer slowly, silently, with his right hand, all the while holding the newspaper in front of him with the left. His hands had become more agile, as if they had multiplied, and his senses were more acute. Everything was vibrating inside him, like a thin wire stretched taut. The atavistic peasant instinct to be wary, watchful, suspicious, to expect the worst and recognise it, had been re-awakened in him and was reaching fever pitch.

The superintendent finished polishing his pistol, reloaded it, gripped it and pretended to aim at the light, at a calendar, at a door handle. But by the time he had suddenly pointed it at the sergeant and fired, the sergeant had already thrown himself to the floor, together with his chair, whipped away the newspaper with his left hand to reveal the pistol he had taken from the drawer, and fired straight at the superintendent's heart. The superintendent collapsed onto the documents in front of him, drenching them in blood.

'He was a good shot,' the sergeant said, looking at the bullet hole behind his desk, 'but I did warn him': almost as if he had beaten him in a contest. But immediately afterwards, the tears came and his teeth started chattering.

14

'Let's sum up,' the commissioner said. 'Let's sum up and then decide... Or rather, the prosecutor will decide. We're going to have the press at our doors soon.'

The commissioner's office. The colonel of Carabinieri was there, too, and in front of them, like a defendant in court, the sergeant.

'Let's sum up, then... According to the sergeant's account, which is full of convincing elements, clues which I confess I was wrong not to consider as I should have, these are the facts, and I'll try to be brief. On the evening of the eighteenth, a call comes into headquarters from Signor Roccella: he asks if someone can go to his house and take a look at something. The sergeant says that someone will go as soon as possible. He tells the superintendent about the phone call and offers to go himself, but the superintendent says he doesn't believe Signor Roccella has come back after all these years; in his opinion, it's a hoax. He tells the sergeant to drop by the following day, and leaves, saying that for the whole of the next day, the festival of Saint Joseph, he will be incommunicado – which in fact he was... It's quite likely that he informed his accomplices of Signor Roccella's unexpected return, and even likelier that he went there in person, got him to open up by telling him he was a police superintendent, sat down next to him at the desk, where Roccella was starting to write about the painting he had found, noticed to his surprise that there was a gun on the desk, and when the moment was right picked it up in his gloved hand and shot him in the head. Then he put a full stop after the words *I've found* and left, closing the door, which had a spring lock, behind him... I must say in self-criticism that when the sergeant pointed out how odd that full stop after *I've found* was, I didn't take much notice. As far as I was concerned, Roccella was out of his mind, he saw suicide as the only way out of his problems, but wanted to kill himself with the police watching... The body would certainly have been discovered the next day, which meant that the house had to be cleared. The whole gang was summoned that night, and the painting and the materials from their clandestine activities were moved.'

'Where?' the magistrate asked.

'In the sergeant's opinion, and mine, too, to the station at Monterosso. The stationmaster and the engineer were part of the gang, probably on the margins, as dealers... Seeing all that stuff arriving, which could have compromised them, the stationmaster and the workman must have got scared. They protested, perhaps made threats, and were killed. They were already dead by the time the Volvo driver arrived at the station, that was why the gang had to get out of there in a hurry... The Volvo driver didn't see the stationmaster and the engineer, he saw their killers... We established that when we showed him the photographs of the stationmaster and the engineer: he'd never seen them before... Then there was the episode of the light switch: the sergeant wasn't the only person to be struck by that.'

'What an idiot!' the magistrate said – his funeral oration for the superintendent. Then, 'But my dear commissioner, my dear colonel, this isn't enough... What if we turned the story on its head? What if the sergeant is lying, and he himself did the things he's accused the superintendent of doing?'

The commissioner and the colonel exchanged glances, saying with their eyes what they had said in words a few days earlier: 'Oh, God!' and 'Unbelievable!'

'It isn't possible,' they both said. Then the commissioner asked the sergeant to leave the room. 'Go into the waiting room, we'll call you in five minutes.'

It was almost half an hour before they called him back.

'Accident,' the magistrate said.

'Accident,' the commissioner said.

'Accident,' the colonel said.

And so the newspaper headline read: *Sergeant accidentally kills superintendent while polishing his pistol.*

While the mortuary chapel was being prepared for the superintendent at headquarters – he would be buried with full honours – the Volvo driver, who had been released from prison, was taken there to complete the bureaucratic formalities which would finally set him free.

Having discharged these, he was just leaving, dishevelled and nervously cheerful, when he passed Father Cricco in the doorway, wearing a tricorn, a surplice and a stole, on his way to bless the corpse.

Father Cricco stopped him with a gesture. 'I think I know you,' he said. 'Are you from my parish?'

'What parish?' the man said. 'I don't have a parish.' And he happily rushed out.

He found his Volvo in the car park, with a parking ticket stuck to it. But he was feeling so pleased, he merely laughed.

He sang as he drove out of town. But after a while, grim-faced and anxious again, he abruptly stopped the car. 'That priest,' he said to himself. 'That priest. I would have recognised him immediately if he hadn't been dressed as a priest: he was the stationmaster, or the man I thought was the stationmaster.'

He considered turning round and going back to headquarters. But a moment later he thought, 'Why should I go looking for trouble again, even more trouble than before?'

And he resumed his homeward journey, singing.

Candido

or A dream dreamed in Sicily

How, where and on what night
Candido Munafò was born;
and why he was named Candido.

Candido Munafò was born in a cave that gaped broad and deep at the foot of a hill of olive trees on the night of July 9th to 10th 1943. It was easy enough to be born in a cave or a stable that summer, and especially that night, with Sicily being fought over by the US seventh army under General Patton, the British eighth army under General Montgomery, the German Hermann Goering division, and a few scattered, almost invisible Italian regiments. It was in fact that very night, with the sky over the island sinisterly illumined by multicoloured Bengal lights and the town ploughed by bombs, that the armies of Patton and Montgomery landed.

In other words, there was nothing supernatural, no premonitory sign, in the fact that Candido Munafò was born in a cave, nor in the fact that this cave was in the area known as Serradifalco, the mountain of the falcon, a place from which to spread your wings and fly off in search of prey; let alone the fact that all that night the sky was lit by rockets, now glowing red, now dazzling white, and echoed with a vast metallic stridulation, as if the night sky itself were made of metal rather than the planes flying across it, their invisible trajectories ending in clusters of explosions, some distant, some closer. The one thing that was marked by fate – that is, by the events that were to take place in Sicily and Italy, starting that night – was the name he was given: heavy with fate, even. If he had been born twelve hours earlier, in the town, which had not been bombed at that point, his name would have been Bruno, after Mussolini's son, who had met his death as an aviator and who lived on in the hearts of all Italians like the lawyer Munafò and his wife Maria Grazia Munafò, née Cressi, the daughter of General Arturo

Cressi of the Fascist militia, hero of the wars in Ethiopia and Spain and slightly less of a hero, thanks to the rheumatism from which he suffered, of the war currently in progress. But, as he was born after the first, terrible bombardment of the town where they lived, his parents chose instead the name Candido: a name his father hit upon in a sudden, almost surreal manner, and which was accepted by Signora Maria Grazia for not entirely noble reasons, for example that she had been so opposed to the original choice, Bruno, as to almost give up on the whole idea. The name Candido was like a blank page: a page on which, now that Fascism had been erased, they would have to learn to write a new life. That there was a book of that name, and a character who wandered through wars between the Abares and the Bulgars, the Jesuits and the kingdom of Spain, was a fact of which the lawyer Francesco Maria Munafò was totally unaware; as was the existence of François-Marie Arouet, who had created that character. It was equally unknown to his wife, even though she had read a few books, unlike her husband who had never read any at all apart from those set at school or those he needed for his profession. As both had been through elementary school, high school and university without ever hearing of Voltaire or Candide, this is hardly surprising: it still happens.

The name Candido exploded inside the lawyer Munafò's mind as soon as the explosions of that first terrible bombardment of the town in which he lived were over. He was near the railway station when it had suddenly begun, about four in the afternoon. He was almost running to catch the train for Palermo, where, the following day, he would have to prove the innocence of a murderer in court. And now, suddenly, it was as if he were inside a corolla, of which the tremendous, almost concentric explosions were the petals. He threw himself, or was thrown, to the ground, the briefcase with the papers for the trial clutched to his chest. Ten minutes later – that, he was to learn, was how long the bombardment lasted – he got back on his feet amid a terrible, stunned silence: a silence that was raining dust, thick, endless dust. At first, he was almost blind: it was the crying, the tears, which opened his eyes to that rain of dust. When, after what seemed a long time, the dust started to disperse, he saw that the street was gone, the railway station was gone, the town was gone. He moved outside the corolla, sliding down into the vast trench surrounding the area and clambering his way out again. He found himself face to face with a grotesque plaster statue, in which only the eyes were alive, as if they had just been horribly ripped from a living man and transplanted onto the statue. For a while he was on the verge of madness, until he recognised himself from the briefcase he was still clutching to his chest and realised that he was looking into a mirror that had rained down almost intact from one of the houses that were now gone. And he found himself uttering, then repeating, over and over, the word *candido*. That was how he came back to an awareness of who he was, where he was, what had happened: through that word. *Candido*, *candido*: the whiteness in which he felt himself caked, the sense of rebirth that was starting to well up inside him.[1] And, still repeating the word, he tore himself from that stupid, stupefied contemplation of himself in the dusty mirror, feeling a sudden pang of anxiety, as painful as a wound he had not previously noticed, about what might have happened to his wife, to the child that was due to be born any day now, and to his house. Unfortunately, he had no idea which way his house was: moving at the speed at which you might imagine a plaster statue would move, he went first one way then the other. Around him, he began hearing moans and cries for help.

He wandered without knowing where he was going until a patrol of soldiers emerged out of the rubble, led by a very young officer. Confronted by that plaster statue, the soldiers laughed nervously. The officer asked him where he was going and what he was looking for. The lawyer told him the name of the street where he lived, and his own name. The officer took a map of the town from the bag he had over his shoulder and, pointing across the smoking wreckage of the railway station, indicated the direction the lawyer had to take to get to his house, and wished him good luck in finding it. 'Thank you,' the lawyer said, and set off through the rubble.

After a couple of hours, he found his house. It was intact, but all the doors and the windows were open, almost torn from their frames. His wife and the maid were leaning wearily against a corner, saying their prayers. The lawyer said a couple, too. Then they filled two suitcases with linen, grabbed their jewellery, money and cheque books, and joined the flood of people escaping out into the countryside.

They were in luck. On the way out of town, they came across a column of military lorries, parked in the shade of the trees, and everyone ran and climbed onto them. When the captain in charge ordered his soldiers to throw them off, the mob, especially the women, threatened to gouge his eyes out and turn him into mincemeat. The captain considered the situation: his soldiers were greatly outnumbered by the furious women. He gave orders to get moving. 'Where are we going?' the soldiers asked. 'Wherever the road takes us,' replied the chorus of women. It seemed a sensible answer, given the circumstances. The lorries set off. They had gone about twenty kilometres when a double line of those terrible American planes appeared, gleaming in the twilight. They would have been beautiful to watch, swooping down so low you might have thought they were going to land, if it were not for the fact that they were scattering machine-gun fire. The lorries came to an abrupt halt, and everyone ran, screaming in terror.

By the time the machine-gun fire stopped and the planes disappeared, the lorries were all in flames. Three or four people were dead, but no one took any notice. Four hours later, in the cave they had discovered in the middle of that landscape, Candido Munafò was born.

How the lawyer Munafò began
to doubt that he was Candido's father;
and the troubles that ensued.

Having brought Candido into the world in front of a hundred women bustling about in a cave (a situation which a colleague of the lawyer Munafò's who was among the fugitives likened to that of the Norman Queen Constance, who gave birth to the Emperor Frederick in a tent in the main square of Jesi, surrounded by many women), Signora Maria Grazia Munafò, née Cressi, became, in the opinion of her husband the lawyer, *a different woman*. In the judgement of her male friends, more beautiful. In that of her female friends – and their judgement was close to her husband's – harder-faced and harder in personality, more irritable and more irritating, sharper-tongued and less attentive to others. As a result, by Christmas that year she had more male friends than female ones. And it was quite obvious that this was making the lawyer Munafò uneasy and bad-tempered.

But even though Maria Grazia felt like *a different woman*, her body alive and buzzing with appetites, like a beehive dripping with honey, it did not cross her mind that she could choose one of those male friends for the kind of furtive love affair in which so many of her female friends, or ex-friends, indulged. Men interested her more than women for one very simple reason: because men were involved in politics, and right now she needed men who were involved in politics. Since the night Candido had been born, her father, General Arturo Cressi, had considered himself, or wished to be considered, a dead man. He had died of fear and out of fear: but his daughter, who loved him very much, thought that he considered himself dead, and wished to be considered as such, because the fatherland was dead, Fascism was dead, and Mussolini had ended up a prisoner of the Germans. She therefore made an effort to bring – as she put it – a spark of life back into the general's eye (he only had one, having lost the other in some heroic action, no one was sure where) which had been extinguished by fear, but also, she thought, by disappointment and disdain. And she chose the right path: the very one the general himself would have chosen if he had been less afraid.

The general's most pressing fear was that the Americans would deport him to North Africa, as they were doing with all those who were denounced to them as dangerous Fascists. Maria Grazia immediately found a way to make this possibility impossible. Thanks to Candido, it should be said. It was the first and only time that Candido was of use to anyone in his family. Since his mother had decided not to breastfeed him, as almost all mothers did at that time, she tried first to give him ass's milk, which was considered very light and delicious by all those who had never drunk it. Candido refused it. She then tried diluted goat's milk: but it was an effort to get him to swallow it, then, once he had swallowed it, to stop him regurgitating it. There were no cows left anywhere in the surrounding area. The lawyer Munafò was therefore forced to go back on his decision to maintain an attitude of patriotic dignity towards the victorious enemy: he went to see the American captain who was in charge of everything and everyone in the town, and told him about Candido's condition, writhing and whimpering with hunger, especially at night; and their condition, too, his and Maria Grazia's, Candido's anxious, sleepless parents. Touched by this story, the captain had powdered milk, condensed milk, semi-condensed milk, sugar, coffee, cornflakes, malt biscuits and canned meat sent to his house. True abundance, even for a house with a larder as well stocked as the Munafò's'.

The lawyer went back to see the captain, to thank him. And this time the captain, perhaps because he had less to do, took him into his confidence. He spoke to him as what he was – a professor of Italian literature at a university – rather than as the captain known to the whole town, with his almost absolute and sometimes capricious powers. He talked about his mother, and showed the lawyer a coloured photograph of her. His mother was Sicilian, and came from a village only fifteen kilometres away, although she could not remember if she still had any relatives there. The lawyer would be able to find them from the surname: he knew the village well. They chatted happily like this for a couple of hours. When the lawyer got home, he uttered to his wife, as a kind of epigraph to his account of his conversation with the captain, the profound truth that had been revealed to him during that conversation. 'It really is a small world,' he said. The soldiers who were dying at that moment, thousands of kilometres from their country, were unlikely to have been of the same opinion, but Signora Munafò shared it immediately. And she decided she would make the world even smaller by inviting Captain John H. Dykes to lunch. The H. stood for Hamlet: a revelation that so enchanted Maria Grazia that, once they were on sufficiently familiar terms, she ended up simply calling the captain Amleto. Which greatly pleased the captain: his mother, he said, always called him that.

Even before Captain John H. Dykes became Amleto in the Munafò household, the general had come back to life. To be exact: the second time the captain came to lunch at his daughter's house. The third time, the general was also there. The general's Fascist past, which they made no attempt to hide, actually made a favourable impression on the captain. His mother had always told him that it was thanks to Fascism that Italians abroad had gained a degree of respect.

Once the nightmare of deportation had receded, Maria Grazia set about the task of getting her father into politics: things were starting to move on that front, even though the

Americans had banned all political activity. The general had a certain inclination towards the Communists, recalling something Mussolini had once confided in him, in about 1930. 'Dear Arturo,' the Duce had said – and whenever the general recalled those words, he filled that 'dear Arturo' with infinite familiarity – 'dear Arturo, if Fascism collapses, there's nothing left but Communism.' In addition, one of the regular visitors to the Munafò household was the lawyer Baron Paolo di Sales, who had been the general's aide-de-camp during the war in Spain, who had written a book on that war (*The Flower of Carmen and the Fasces*), and who was now said to be, *in pectore*,[2] the secretary of the local Communist Party. But Maria Grazia would not allow a good word to be said for the Communist Party, not with Amleto in the house. Either the Christian Democrats or the Liberals: those were the only two parties between which it was fitting for the general to choose. The general overcame the repugnance he felt for priests by remembering that in Spain he had fought for the faith of Christ, and chose the Christian Democrats.

While Maria Grazia was constructing her father's new political fortune, Candido, who had been dark-skinned during the early days of his life, was growing pink and blond, thanks to the milk and other wonderful American foodstuffs. He looked more and more like John H. Dykes – Amleto (although the lawyer Munafò, with surly obstinacy, continued to call him *Ggionn*). This ever more striking resemblance, and the ease and familiarity which had been established between Maria Grazia and Amleto, upset the lawyer Munafò so much that there began to grow inside him, obscurely, like a tumour, a thought that could not be called a thought, a suspicion that could not be called a suspicion, a feeling that could not be called a feeling. At the rare times when he caught a glimpse of what it was, he laughed at himself, mocked himself, called himself crazy. But the tumour was there, and growing. And it was this: that John H. Dykes was Candido's father, or at least that he, Francesco Maria Munafò, wasn't Candido's father. It was pure madness: not only because, when Candido had been conceived, Professor John H. Dykes had been teaching college in Helena, Montana, but also, and above all, because Maria Grazia had never made love (and then only in a manner of speaking, as we shall see) with any man other than her husband the lawyer.

The outcome was constant quarrels, which the lawyer, unwilling to confess the obscure reason, even to himself, provoked on extremely trivial pretexts. And even though appearances were always saved – in front of Amleto, their other friends, and the general – the peace of the Munafò household had been shattered. Maria Grazia would call her husband a yokel and a Mafioso, alluding to his not very distant peasant origins and his professional activities, which were not exactly spotlessly clean, and the lawyer would respond by calling her a flirt: and each time it cost him a mental effort, accompanied by a nervous twitch, to use the word *flirt* instead of the word *whore* which was welling up inside him.

How Amleto left and returned;
and what happened, deservedly, to the lawyer
Munafò and, undeservedly, to Candido.

John H. Dykes left immediately after the Christmas holidays, which for the Munafò household, thanks to the support of the American military, had been replete with food and drink.

Once Amleto had gone, the lawyer felt relatively calm. Only the sight of Candido, who looked ever more like Amleto, troubled him; and once, when Maria Grazia, in all innocence, in a moment when her husband wanted peace and not war, said, 'Don't you think he looks a lot like Amleto?' the lawyer felt himself being lifted on wings of madness, that is, those wings made him lift a corner of the table cloth on which plates, glasses and cutlery had been laid for lunch, and tug it violently towards him. The sudden, impetuous act, the crash, and the broken crockery and spilt wine and sauce that lay on the floor left Maria Grazia stunned and terrified for a moment. This was followed by a flood of words and tears. The lawyer, who could not and would not explain the reason for his gesture, but at the same time felt himself, still obscurely, to be in the right for having made it, and therefore entitled not to apologise, escaped to the countryside, where he remained for two days. When he returned, he found that his wife had put up a wall of silence around her. The person who showed her anger with the lawyer in no uncertain terms was the maid: always a loyal ally of the signora.

Maria Grazia's impenetrable silence was explained by the fact that she had come to a decision: to leave a man whom, as she now realised in self-justification, she had never loved and who, moreover, seemed to be in the grip of a madness he had previously managed to hide but now had no hesitation in manifesting. He was torturing her. And enjoying it.

Maria Grazia was twenty-four years old and had a great hunger to love and to be loved, to have fun, and to see the world. She asked herself how much she really loved Candido, and decided she did not love him very much at all, despite his resemblance to Amleto. If she left the child, none of her friends or acquaintances would forgive her: but she found sufficient reasons to forgive herself. The traumatic circumstances in which Candido had been born somehow worked in her to make the sacrifice less tragic, the separation less painful. On the other hand, she had to think of the general: she did not want her abandonment of what the code called 'the matrimonial home' to harm his chances with the Catholic party, since things seemed at the moment to be going in the right direction. She had to do things correctly: by making judicious use of the Catholic party, the priests and the Church. Even if there had been divorce in Italy, Maria Grazia would still have preferred to free herself from her husband by seeking an annulment from the ecclesiastical court, however long and humiliating the process. Humiliating because of all the things, true and false, which she would have to say about her own body, and which other people would say about her. Which in this case (the line chosen by specialised lawyers and by clergymen highly experienced in such matters), was that, as soon as her husband touched her, she would freeze and then faint: so that it was as if her husband were venting his desire on a dead woman, when he didn't simply lose heart at the first attempt. It was getting to be partly true anyway; an objective confirmation, on Munafò's part, of the despair which had worked its way insanely into him and which, now no longer in the abstract, but based on fact, was growing and blinding him with anger. He was almost always in the country now; while Maria Grazia, feeling freer, surrounded by lawyers and clergymen, and always accompanied by the general, was setting in motion the annulment of her marriage.

During Munafò's absence, Amleto returned on a two-week furlough. He arrived like a husband, a true husband, the true husband. Although there had not been any contact between them that went beyond a handshake (the handshake when they parted had been longer and more tremulous than most) or any understanding that went beyond looks that were either tenderly joyful or sadly trusting, when Amleto set foot once more in the Munafò household they embraced, kissed on the cheeks and then, after a moment of luminous hesitation, for a long time on the mouth. Just like in a film, Maria Grazia thought at that moment: an American film. And everything happened so simply, so spontaneously, that undressing and getting into bed and making love was in the natural order of things, the natural order of existence, of being alive. And so, for the first time, Maria Grazia knew love. Her joy was shared by the maid, even though for different reasons: for the maid, whose name was Concetta, the joy mainly consisting of the fact that at last she could actually call the lawyer Munafò a *cuckold* whenever she wanted, at least mentally.

In the next room, Candido was following the flight of cherubs and roses painted on the ceiling. That ceiling was his universe. He was a very calm child.

How the lawyer Munafò and Candido both faced solitude.

The process to annul the marriage was, as predicted, a long one. The outcome was certain, that is, that the annulment would be granted, but there was so much sensitive, delicate material to be carefully sifted through that it all naturally took a long time. The lawyer Munafò raised no objection: it was perfectly true that Maria Grazia had never loved him (to the extent, as he thought but did not say, that she had given birth to a child who resembled the man she would later meet and love), very true that she froze when he caressed her, her eyes glazed over and she lost consciousness. And so the process dragged on, unavoidably long-drawn-out.

In the meantime, Maria Grazia had moved, first to her father's house, then to another town, where, it was said, she was lodging in a convent. In fact, she was moving from one town to another, wherever Amleto was posted; but furtively, in order not to compromise the outcome of the trial and out of respect for the man who, in the eyes of the law, was still her husband. He was also due some respect for the way he had been conducting himself before the ecclesiastical court: correctly, loyally. Now he, too, could not wait to be freed from the bonds of matrimony: even though he had no intention of remarrying, and had even become somewhat misogynistic. Solitude was smiling on him, a solitude that would be sealed by a ruling from an ecclesiastical court and recognised by a court of the Italian State. There was only one complication: Candido. Both husband and wife felt under an obligation, imposed on them by the society in which their relatives, their friends, the priests and the lawyers lived, to keep up a terrible pretence: they had to pretend that they wanted him and that neither was prepared to yield him to the other.

If there had been a King Solomon to decide whether Candido should be entrusted to the father or the mother, the poor child might have been cut in half: such was the stubbornness demonstrated by both father and mother in their desire to keep him. Fortunately for Candido, the moment of decision finally came in November 1945, involving a good-natured judge from the mainland, lawyers, priests, and the chorus of relatives and friends. And besides, the decision, difficult as it was, had been a foregone conclusion from the moment Maria Grazia had set the procedure in motion: Candido had to stay with his father, mainly for the reason – a reason recognised by everyone, including the women – that a woman who refused to resign herself to staying until death did them part with a husband she did not love and who did not love her deserved to be punished. And what better punishment could there be than this: to be deprived forever of her own child? The fact that the very opposite was the case – that it was a punishment for the husband to keep Candido, and one more freedom for Maria Grazia to give him up – did not matter: what mattered was to confirm the rule and keep up appearances.

The lawyer Munafò, in accordance with the rules and appearances, made a show of being vindictively happy, vindictively satisfied to have won the battle for custody of Candido; and Maria Grazia painfully defeated to have lost it. In fact, the real loser was the lawyer: forced to keep a child he did not love, a child he didn't even feel was his own, a child whom, shamefully, in his secret rage, he did not call Candido, but *the American*.

Ever pinker, ever blonder, ever calmer and more contented, Candido did not feel the slightest sting from the nest of thorns in which he found himself. It seemed as if he could quite happily have done without a mother or a father. The one person he could not do without, for his most vital and immediate needs, was Concetta, who was still in charge of providing a mother's love, in defiance of the lawyer Munafò; but not even towards Concetta did he demonstrate an attachment that went beyond the benefits of eating, drinking and other needs, such as the pleasures of hide and seek, which Concetta sometimes played with him. A game which, it has to be said, delighted Candido for no more than ten minutes, before he abandoned it and returned to his own secret, solitary games. These consisted – we can only attempt to define them approximately – of a kind of crossword puzzle, only with things. Just as adults played with crosswords, Candido played with cross things. Words also came into it, almost always the first and last syllables of the words, but it was above all things, their place, the uses they could be put to, their shape, their colour, their weight, their consistency, that helped to develop the game and give it the pleasant sense of difficulty, the pleasant sense of chance that it needed.

The greatest praise that Concetta could give Candido was that 'wherever you put him, he'll stay'. He could stay with other children, unless they were violent, and he could be alone and stay still for hours on end in whatever place Concetta left him. He had an innate gentleness, and at the same time, if such a thing can be said of a child, a kind of formality. He was self-sufficient, that was it. According to Concetta – who was a very nervous person – he was a child without nerves. 'You would never guess he was born that terrible night,' she would say. But she also thought that that terrible night had given birth to someone who was, if not stupid, a little slow, a little foggy in his mind. And whenever she thought this, she would love him even more and would call him *my darling, my baby, my boy*. Candido would respond to these effusions with a gentle smile which would turn tolerant whenever Concetta smothered him with kisses. He didn't like to be smothered with kisses, but he tolerated it. He also tolerated his grandfather's kisses, which made him slightly uncomfortable because of the general's goatee beard: the only thing that had remained unchanged about the former hero of the Fascist wars who had become a Christian Democrat, a republican, and of course, an anti-Fascist.

Whenever his political activities left him time, the general would go to see Candido, or would have Concetta bring him over to his house. Despite being given sesame and raisin biscuits, which he liked, Candido was very bored at his grandfather's. After the day the general took down one of the many rifles that hung on the walls of his house and took him out into the garden and showed him how to load and fire it, whenever Concetta announced, 'We're going to see your grandfather the general,' Candido would firmly say 'no' and, if Concetta insisted, his eyes would fill with tears. Which was enough to make her back down. 'All right, my darling, we won't go. If you don't want to go, we won't go.' And she would wonder, 'But what did that awful old man do to him?' because if Candido didn't like something, even if the dislike seemed unfounded and incomprehensible, there had to be a reason for it and she decided to dislike it, too.

Once, when the general complained that she no longer brought Candido to see him, and that he had started to miss these visits, Concetta was forced to tell him that the decision was Candido's and that it was unshakeable. 'But why?' the general asked. 'How should I know?' Concetta replied. 'You should know.' This reply made the general fly off the handle, but, when he calmed down and remembered the last time Candido had been brought to see him and he had shown him how to fire a rifle, he pronounced this disdainful verdict on Candido: 'He's chicken.'

How Candido became to all intents and purposes an orphan; and how he ran the risk of relocating to Helena, Montana.

By the time he was five, Candido knew almost everything about the lawyer Munafò, but the lawyer knew nothing about Candido, nor did he care to know anything. The child had plenty of food and toys, and was washed and dressed as required. What more could be asked of a father who, supposedly if not absolutely definitely, was like Joseph son of Jacob, whose wife had conceived by virtue of the Holy Spirit, just as Maria Grazia had conceived by virtue of the American Spirit? There was never the slightest reason to reprimand Candido; if only there were, the lawyer thought at times, darkly. He never had to be urged or cajoled to eat: the child had a good appetite and was even judiciously greedy. He never had to be forbidden to play dangerous games: he did not like them. He never had to be forced to go to sleep at the times when he was supposed to, never refused or protested, and he would fall asleep as soon as his head hit the pillow; 'like an angel,' as Concetta put it.

Candido, then, knew everything about his father. He did not know his thoughts, but he did know everything relating to his profession, how much money he made from both his profession and his properties, his relationships with his clients, his colleagues, the judges, the tenant farmers and farm workers. He knew him the way President Nixon's tape recorders knew everything President Nixon said. Except that Nixon knew about the tape recorders and the lawyer Munafò did not know that Candido was listening: which, considering the disasters that befell both of them, suggests that Munafò was less of a fool than Nixon.

Candido had got into the habit of slipping into his father's office: every afternoon at the hour of vespers, when the light,

60

intense everywhere else in the house, took on a soft, vaporous, somnolent feel in that room with its heavy, dark furniture, its dark leather armchairs, its dark damask drapes. Candido would go behind a large sofa, lie down on the thick carpet which covered almost the entire floor, and from there would tirelessly explore the paintings on the ceiling; and sometimes, staring up now at one, now at another of the naked women flying across it, he would feel sleep come down on him like one of those pale blue veils waved by the women or ruffled by the wind, and soon fall into a delicious slumber. The ceilings of the bedrooms were his textbooks: from cherubs and roses he had graduated to naked women and veils.

Whenever he happened to fall asleep, as lightly and gently as a veil lovingly abandoned to him by one of the women up there, almost always the one who was his favourite, he would wake up when his father entered and opened the windows and sat down at his desk. He would not move, however, but would stay where he was and wait for the visitors to arrive. If he got bored after that, he would slide silently on his stomach, hidden from his father's sight by the furniture, towards the only one of the three doors to the office through which no one ever entered or went out, which like the others was hidden by the heavy drapes. But he did not often get bored: it was a kind of invisible theatre, and he liked listening to the conversations, the different tones and volumes of the voices, the dramatic or imploring or persuasive tones they assumed, the peasants' Sicilian, his father's Italian. It should be said that there was no hint of malice in his eavesdropping: keeping silent and sliding out of the room were merely moves in a game he was playing with himself.

This game, aesthetic or – one step down – sensual in nature, rarely aroused in Candido any interest in the actual things that were being talked about: either because those things were talked about in a poor, incoherent way, or because, even when they were talked about very well by the people involved or their relatives, and even when they were clearly summarised by his father, they almost never made any sense to Candido: luckily for the lawyer Munafò and his clients. But their luck couldn't last forever; and in fact it didn't.

One afternoon, Candido found himself listening to someone confessing to a murder. He had heard about that murder from Concetta: with fright and abhorrence. Then he had heard it being talked about by his companions at kindergarten, especially by the son of a lieutenant in the Carabinieri who was very proud of the fact that it was his father who had arrested the killer. That afternoon, however, in his father's office, he learned instead that the man the lieutenant had arrested was not the killer, he was someone who might well have had his reasons to kill the victim, but did not have reasons as serious, although covert and secret, as those of the man who had really committed the murder. Candido did not have any clear idea about killing, dying, death. Or rather, he had the same idea as Concetta, that is, that it was a kind of journey, like leaving one place to go to another. The confession which that man made to his father, in the course of asking for advice on what to do in the event of the innocent man's innocence being recognised and the Carabinieri's suspicions falling on him, impressed Candido to the extent that he longed to know what impression such a revelation would make on the lieutenant's son. So he made sure he recorded that conversation in his mind, including the name of the murderer. And the next day he promptly revealed it to his classmates at the kindergarten: which told the lieutenant's son that his father had made a mistake. And just as promptly the lieutenant's son criticised his father: which made him lose face among his colleagues, for arresting the innocent instead of the guilty.

This caused a great fuss. The Carabinieri arrived in force at the kindergarten, and in the presence of the principal and some of the teachers made Candido tell them everything. Candido related in detail everything he had heard in his father's office, pleased to be the centre of attention of all these Carabinieri who seemed to be pleased to be listening to him.

When he left the kindergarten, he found Concetta waiting for him as usual; but looking uglier than usual, because she had been doing a lot of weeping and even now could barely hold back her tears. She told him his father had gone away on a very long journey. The news would have been greeted by Candido with the usual indifference – his father was always going somewhere: the country, Palermo, Rome – if Concetta had not had that weepy face and had not added a sentence which made no sense to Candido but rather scared him. 'I ought to cut your tongue out,' Concetta said.

He then learned a few rather vague details about his father's departure. Apparently (he never found out precisely, nor did he really want to), once the Carabinieri had left, the principal of the kindergarten had lost no time in informing the lawyer Munafò what Candido had told the Carabinieri: and the lawyer, feeling like an outcast, both from his profession and from the rules by which he had lived until then, had put an end to his own life. It was his way of trying to re-establish the rules which Candido had unwittingly infringed: he wrote that he was killing himself because he was tired, and because he was ill, perhaps with cancer, perhaps with his nerves. A noble lie, which did not stop the client whose confession Candido had reported from being sentenced to twenty-seven years' imprisonment.

In the meantime, that same day, Concetta took Candido to the general's house. And there the boy stayed until his mother arrived; an arrival which marked for Candido the beginning of a whole month of tribulations, since his mother had come believing it her duty to take her son back with her to Helena, where she now lived as Mrs John H. Dykes.

Candido liked this woman who was his mother. He thought she looked like his favourite of the nudes on the ceiling. And he would have liked it (Stendhal!) if, when she took him in her arms and hugged him, there were no clothes between her and him. But as far as going to America with her was concerned, that was quite another matter. He wanted to stay with Concetta, in the house with the nice paintings. His tears, and a desperate attempt to run away (they found him wandering the countryside, hungry and ragged) convinced his mother to leave him there. A decision, it must be said, which was a relief for her, too. But, as she was saying goodbye to him, and he was coldly returning her kisses, she whispered to her father, 'He's a little monster.' It was a thought that had already occurred to the general.

How Candido was wretchedly blamed by the general, the relatives and almost the whole town; and how he reacted when he became aware of the fact.

A month before the lawyer Munafò killed himself, the general had been elected to the National Parliament; and with so many preferential votes, on the Christian Democrat list, as to surpass every other candidate in the west of Sicily. At the beginning of the campaign, his opponents had tried to attack him for his past as a Fascist warmonger: but these attacks made the crowds that came to the general's meetings feel a certain admiration for him; and besides, the general had threatened to counterattack by giving the names, positions and incomes of the Fascists standing for other parties, of whom there were many. The local Communist Party candidate was Baron Paolo Di Sales who, as we have said, had been the general's aide-de-camp during the Spanish war: his most direct opponent, therefore, in the election campaign. But they both behaved with discretion and grace, and even managed to come out with expressions of mutual respect and esteem: at least in public. And the Baron was elected, too.

At the last meeting the general held, Concetta, more of a fanatical propagandist for the party of the Cross than for the general who represented that party, took Candido along. Candido soon became bored and disgusted. There were too many people, too many voices, too much drunken breath; he could smell it because of all the people who felt obliged to bend over and stroke him and ask him if he was pleased that his grandfather the general was going to become a deputy. Candido did not know what a deputy was, and anyway he didn't give a damn if his grandfather became one or not.

Once elected, a personal triumph in the overall triumph of the Christian Democrats that April 18th 1948, it was as if the general had been rejuvenated. He had already started to wear a black bandage over his bad eye during the campaign, and now, rejuvenated as he was by his electoral success, it gave him a predatory, piratical air which appealed to the Ladies of the Sacred Heart, the Ursulines and the Daughters of Mary. In his renewed confidence and self-assurance, when he spoke of his former son-in-law (former in two ways: because of the ecclesiastical court and because of his death), the general would say, 'He was an idiot: if he had come straight to me, I would have fixed everything.' And if he happened to say it when Candido was present, he would give the boy a glance that was a mixture of scorn and commiseration.

The other relatives looked at him in the same way – those on his father's side with less commiseration – as, when they met him, did the men who had been his father's friends and the women who had been his mother's friends. Only Concetta, after the words she had blurted out about cutting out his tongue, looked at him without a hint of reproach and with abundant, tearful piety. To be honest, Concetta's absolute piety made Candido more uncomfortable than everyone else's ambiguous feelings. In other words, they all made him uncomfortable, some more than others: but Concetta more than anyone. He therefore began observing her, studying her. He soon realised that Concetta's feelings about the dead lawyer Munafò had changed radically, and that the new feelings, almost of worship, went hand in hand with remorse for having once felt ran-cour and mockery. Simultaneously, her feelings about Signora Maria Grazia had changed, too. This was something Candido could neither know nor guess, but the insult of *cuckold*, which Concetta had many times bestowed mentally on the lawyer, had now changed to that of *whore*, bestowed just as frequently on the absent signora. The lawyer himself came to her in a dream and thanked her for these changed feelings, and then took the opportunity to ask her to sing a few masses for him: where he was now, he said, he had been abandoned, given up as forgotten.

Concetta told Candido about the request and was silent about the thanks. She also shared with him her deduction and conviction that the lawyer was in purgatory: why would someone who was in hell care about masses? And from that moment on, the masses came thick and fast, to refrigerate the place in purgatory where the lawyer was: and they attended all of them, in the church bedecked for mourning, Concetta praying contritely and frantically; Candido less contritely, and even feeling quite bored and distracted. And it was during one of these masses that Candido, letting his thoughts pursue one another, realised that what made death so terrible wasn't so much that you weren't around anymore, but, on the contrary, that you were still around and at the mercy of the changeable feelings of those who remained: like his father in Concetta's memories, feelings and thoughts. It must be a bother, if you were dead, to still be present in what the living remembered, felt and thought; and even in what they dreamed. In Candido's imagination, it was like an abrupt call to attention, a whistle that blew and made you run, arriving panting and out of breath. What Concetta called *the other life* was really a dog's life.

For his part, Candido was not much disturbed by his father from *the other life* (although, to tell the truth, he thought it rather unlikely that there was one): only in so far as remembering him helped Candido understand why other people looked at him with that mixture of reproach and pity. The pity was something he understood immediately. Or rather, he thought he did, when he saw another parentless child who lived with his grandparents being treated the same way. In fact, as he realised later, the pity they showed towards him was different, complicated by their anxiety as to how it would affect him when he learned, as he would sooner or later, that his father had died because he, Candido, had said something he shouldn't. The reproach, though, took him a lot more time and effort to figure out. Observing Concetta and occasionally provoking her; retaining in his memory everything his grandfather, his relatives and acquaintances said about his father and working on it; going over his memories of the afternoons spent in the office, lying on the rug, hidden by the sofa; and putting everything together, just as he did with that beautiful wooden puzzle they had given him, the single pieces of which he loved – because of their taste, their touch, their smell – more than the picture you could make with them, Candido finally arrived at an image which was not yet a judgement nor as distinct as we are presenting it: the image of his father as a man who makes an account of his whole life, and what it adds up to makes him shoot himself. An image which, innocently, had been crystallised for him by the many times he had seen his father doing his accounts; but to the general, Concetta and all the others it would have appeared to be a product of the most incredible and monstrous cynicism.

But, even though Concetta did not know about this image, when he was about ten Candido began to reveal himself as a monster to her, too, just as, at the age of five, he had revealed himself as such to his mother and grandfather. A monster to whom one ought, in Concetta's opinion, to show more love than if he had been *like any other child*. Candido did not worship his dead father, did not ask for news of his living mother, had no affection for his grandfather, and didn't give a damn about her either. What was more, he said things which made her shudder; and he would say them in a way that had something diabolical about it: laughing shrilly and putting them to music. So it was that one day he said to her, 'You don't want to tell me, but I know I killed my father.' And he turned and ran away, just like a devil: because, according to Concetta, devils always ran like colts, spoke in music, and laughed as if they were sharpening knives.

How the general and Concetta worried about Candido's education; and how the general decided to give him a tutor, just like in the old days.

Several times, Concetta made up her mind to talk to the general about the devilishness of which Candido gave indications; but each time she put it off, with the excuse either that the general was too busy, or that she did not think he would be capable of understanding, or that she needed to wait another week or two to see if Candido changed. The truth was that Concetta was afraid the general would send Candido away to a boarding school. Devil or not, what would her life be without Candido?

Instead of speaking to the general, she went to see the archpriest. And the archpriest, despite Concetta's recommendations, spoke to the general; although obviously not in the terms in which Concetta had spoken to him. The story of the diabolical spirit that had taken up residence in the child, on the one hand made him laugh, and on the other worried him. What worried him was the fact that the child was living with an ignorant woman full of superstitious fears like Concetta. Perhaps what seemed diabolical to Concetta was simply a defence mechanism on Candido's part, a healthy rebellion against her funereal religious zeal, her constant, painstaking worship of the dead and of death, her obscure beliefs and penances.

The archpriest was considered, and considered himself, *modern*. He had devoted a great deal of time to studying psychology; concealing within that word another which could only be uttered cautiously and with many reservations: psychoanalysis. He had even written a treatise on *moral psychology*, in other words, psychoanalysis, the well-organised manuscript of which was now in the bishop's palace waiting for an *imprimatur*, as if it had run aground among the rocks. The rocks were the bishop's inability to decide whether to refuse it or grant it, although leaning more towards refusing it: because not only had he glimpsed the word psychoanalysis behind the word psychology, but he also found extreme and revolutionary the keenly argued theory that the Church should recognise and adopt psychology, in other words, psychoanalysis, as an essential, almost innate, indefeasible element of the ecclesiastical ministry, and therefore not to be left in lay hands. And the only way not to leave it in lay hands was through a kind of spiritual 'coup': granting the status of deacon, whether they wanted it or not, to all those in the Catholic world who exercised the profession of psychologist, in other words, psychoanalyst. Besides, theologically speaking, the figure of the deacon was so vague and ill defined...

Given the archpriest Lepanto's inclinations and studies, it can easily be deduced how much the case of Candido, as Concetta had presented it, would arouse his interest. He therefore spoke about it to the general, and the general confessed to him that he, too, was worried about the child's upbringing and his strange way of thinking. The archpriest offered to look into it: let the boy be sent to him after school, he would help him with his homework, and at the same time would observe him, study him, analyse him.

Candido began to visit the archpriest, and was happy to do so. He enjoyed discovering little by little, in the course of their conversations, what made a priest: that mysterious man, enclosed in his long black robe, who by putting on lace and damask could turn the host into the body of Christ and make it possible for a dead man to rise from purgatory to paradise (powers about which, according to Concetta, it was blasphemy to harbour any doubts; but Candido did). Enclosed in the diving suit of his plans and intrigues, the archpriest felt like an underwater fisherman spying on Candido's images and thoughts, catching them unawares, spiking them, sure they would prove more convincing because of all his plans and intrigues. In reality, it was Candido who was spying on the archpriest and analysing him.

Physically, there was something catlike about Candido, something soft, velvety, indolent: drowsy, dreamy eyes which at moments would narrow and light up with attentiveness; a slow, silent way of moving which at times became agile, although still silent. And his mind was just the same: given to flights of fancy, rambling and eccentric; but always on the alert. And besides, he liked his resemblance to a cat: he liked the freedom he knew he had, his lack of ties to the people around him, his capacity for self-sufficiency. The only tie he felt he had, in fact, was with the house cat: a fine grey cat who was the same age as him, which in cat terms meant he was his grandfather's age. Indeed, as soon as he had learned how to measure the lives of cats, that was what he called him: Grandpa. Something which the general, learning about it by chance, took so badly that he wrote about it to his daughter. 'He calls the cat Grandpa,' he wrote. And his daughter wrote back, jokingly, 'I told you: he's a little monster.'

That he was a little monster was something of which even the archpriest became convinced after a while. In their analysis of each other, the archpriest had not discovered anything that required diagnosis and subsequent therapy; whereas Candido had discovered that the archpriest had a kind of obsession, a somewhat complicated obsession which could approximately be summed up in these words: that all children kill their fathers, and some, sometimes, also kill Our Father in Heaven; except that this is not a real killing, but a kind of game in which instead of things there are names and instead of facts intentions; a game, in short, rather like the mass. Candido did not like the fact that the archpriest thought this of all children, but more for the sake of the archpriest than for the sake of the children. If he also thought it of him, it seemed to Candido, he would, patiently, have to disillusion him. In every way he could, he made it clear to him, sometimes in words, that yes, it may be that all children killed their fathers and Our Father in Heaven: but not him, Candido, oh, no; he had not killed his father and didn't know, and didn't want to know, anything about that other Father.

This attitude of Candido's upset the archpriest and faced him with a crisis of conscience. Because Candido, as far as the archpriest knew, really had killed his father: and therefore he had either to convince him that he had killed him or leave him in that arrogantly innocent state. It was a terrible problem, similar to that encountered by the character in a story by an American writer, who, wishing to prove the theory of probability as expressed in the example of twelve monkeys which, typing at random on twelve typewriters, in the end write all the works in the Library of Congress, bought twelve monkeys and twelve typewriters, and found that the monkeys immediately, not *in the end*, reproduced all of Dante, Shakespeare and Dickens: leaving him with no other alternative than to kill all twelve of them. To really solve the problem, the archpriest would have had to kill Candido: a thought which, it should be said to his credit, never occurred to him. So the problem stayed with him, and he never managed to solve it. But nor did Candido ever manage to solve his problem with the archpriest.

And so, for years, facing each other across a table on which lay a bronze crucifix, a pewter inkpot, the Acts of the Apostles and the works of Freud and Jung, they sat scrutinising each other, spying on each other. They talked of many things, but always, both of them, with that thought in mind. And in this way they ended up liking each other, above and beyond the fathers and Our Father.

How Candido and the archpriest
talked of many things;
and how it upset the general.

Candido always polished off his school homework quickly: at
home, by himself. The archpriest seldom found any mistakes in
it; and whenever he did find one, he never needed to explain it,
since Candido immediately recognised and corrected it. So that
the scholastic part of their encounters was soon exhausted, and
they talked of other things: that is, without the archpriest realising it, the things about which Candido wanted them to talk.

They talked about Concetta and the general; and the archpriest talked about himself, his poverty-stricken childhood, his
mother, his father, his adolescence and youth at the Episcopal
Seminary in the provincial capital, the day he had been ordained,
and the party held in his village to celebrate his ordination.
Whenever they talked about Concetta and the general, it was as
if they were talking about two themes that were behind everything: behind all the error, stupidity and madness in human
life. Candido's image of the two was a fantastic image of them
both wrapped around with funeral creepers which hid them.
The image had come to him from the ivy covering the ruins of
the old church in the cemetery: and he would have liked to see
what ruins were hiding inside Concetta and the general. The
archpriest was happy to talk about Concetta, since Catholics
like Concetta, of whom there were many, were the reason for his
anxiety as a priest: an anxiety that at times came close to despair.
He was reluctant, though, to talk about the general. Having
noted that, for Candido, the general had not taken the place of
his father, just as Concetta had not taken the place of his mother,
he would have preferred, rather than talking to the boy about
the general, to talk to him about that distant mother, married
to a man Candido did not know and the mother of two other

children who were equally unknown to Candido. But, for Candido, his mother and the man she had married and his two American brothers were so distant that he seldom thought about them; and whenever he did happen to think about them, he felt a vague curiosity about their distant and surely very different life, but never anything like a sense of deprivation, or envy, or anger. It could even be said that he felt nothing at all when he thought about that life; indeed, when he began to learn how to write and the archpriest, at the general's suggestion, urged him to write a letter to his mother, it was only out of consideration for the archpriest that he didn't say no. The letter began: 'Dear Signora...' and drily informed her that they were all well: he, Concetta, the cat, the general and the archpriest. The archpriest's first reaction when he read it was to lose his temper; but then, thinking about it again in the light of all that he knew, he found it amusing. 'What? How can you call your mother dear Signora?' Patiently, Candido rewrote the letter, with one variation: dear Mummy. But that was not all: the priest's appetite had been whetted; and it turned to hunger when Candido told him about the naked woman on the ceiling and said that he had the feeling he was writing as a game, a piece of make-believe, to a woman who only existed in that painting. 'So,' the archpriest thought, 'in order to reject his mother, to condemn her for having left him, he has identified her with the naked woman on the ceiling: because his mother, given the idea he has of his mother and the idea he has of nudity, cannot be naked.' He therefore laboured to free Candido of that identification on which he was fixated, but Candido was so insistent that the image of his mother was there, flying across the ceiling, that the archpriest asked to see it.

It was a bit of a shock. The painted lady really did resemble Signora Maria Grazia, so much so that it might be thought she had posed nude for the painter (which was quite impossible, since there, in a corner of the ceiling, beneath the painter's signature, was the date 1904), and this fact provoked a certain unease in the archpriest: in the realm – the delicate, transparent but carefully submerged realm – of the senses. It was hard to tell, from the way Candido himself candidly described it, whether identifying his mother with that naked woman was really an obscure desire on Candido's part to degrade her: contemplating that body, an activity in which he indulged from time to time, was like contemplating a desire purged of all instinct, all feeling, even desire itself: something idyllic, a moment of harmony with the world. The archpriest, on the other hand, felt a strange, unhealthy kind of passion rising up inside him. He decided therefore not to talk any more to Candido about his mother: which was something of a relief to Candido, even though at times it did occur to him to wonder why the archpriest had stopped talking about her. The relief was indeed due to the fact that a subject that was painful to him was no longer being touched upon: but for him, the pain lay in the memory (and in the threat he still felt hanging over him) of the time his mother had come to take him back with her to America.

So they talked instead about Concetta and the general; and the archpriest talked about himself, cleverly urged to do so by Candido. Not that Candido knew he was being clever: he simply felt curious, without any malice, and without any sense of guilt. It was the same curiosity with which he set about learning, as his school demanded, the facts of the past, the climates and produce of distant countries, the three kingdoms of nature (although dividing nature into three kingdoms did not seem natural to him), or solving problems in arithmetic. That was it: the people close to him were like problems; and he wanted to solve them, to polish them off so that he was free of them, just as he polished off the problems they set him at school by solving them. And of these people, of these problems, the most important, after a while, was the general. In other words, Fascism. In other words, that past on whose borderline with the present he had been born.

That line, according to what people said on public holidays, especially the one on April 25th commemorating the liberation of the whole of Italy from Fascism, was like a line separating darkness from light, night from day; and as the general had found himself in the middle, it had cut him in two. That was why, thought Candido, he wore that band over one eye: that was the half of his grandfather that was still in darkness. And the most immediate problem for Candido was this: how could a man who had been cut in two like that carry on living as happily and energetically as the general did? Because there was no doubt about it: half of his grandfather continued to live (or to die, if Fascism was dead) in his past. All the relics he kept in his bedroom proved that: the little triangular gold-fringed flags of marbled silk, black on one side, tricoloured on the other, the medals, the signed photographs of Mussolini, Badoglio,³ Generalisimo Franco (whenever the general said "el Generalisimo", it sounded to Candido as if he was squeezing the first syllables and then savouring a chocolate liqueur with the others).

When Candido presented the archpriest with this problem, this was the solution he was given: in his youth the general had made a mistake, and had continued making the same mistake for twenty years; but since that mistake had involved great sacrifices, not the least of which was losing an eye, he still cherished the few things the fatherland and Fascism had given him in return for those sacrifices. But when he presented the same problem to the general, this indulgent solution roused him to a terrible fit of rage. 'I didn't make a mistake, I've never made a mistake,' he screamed, and launched into a tirade about Fascism which we can sum up thus: Fascism had been great, but the Italians had been small and cowardly (apart, obviously, from General Cressi and a few others). And when his breath failed him, Candido said calmly, 'It was the archpriest who told me you made a mistake.' If he had said that in the first place, the general would have been more cautious: because many of the votes that had sent him to Parliament were due to the archpriest. But he couldn't take back his tirade now. Flushed with silent anger, he walked furiously up and down. Candido took advantage of the silence to ask calmly, 'Did you make a mistake then or are you making a mistake now?' The general stopped in front of him and, visibly making an effort not to give him a good slap, said, 'What do you mean "a mistake", you worm? It's all the same.' And he stormed out of the room.

What struck Candido was not so much the fact that he had been called a worm as the mysterious statement 'it's all the same.' What was the same: present and past, Fascism and anti-Fascism? He asked the archpriest for clarification, reporting word for word what his grandfather had said.

The archpriest was troubled by this. He did not answer Candido's question, but said he would speak to the general. It was clear, though, that he had become angry, and that something was eating away at him.

He did in fact speak to the general. It was not a friendly encounter, to judge by the consequences that conversation had for Candido. The general not only called him a worm again, a creeping worm, a foul worm; but also a spy, a snitch, an informer, a traitor to his kin, a spy and a traitor ever since he was born. Under that hail of words, Candido fell silent. What upset him was that the general threatened to put an end to his after-school sessions with the archpriest.

How Candido did not know that he had power over his closest relative; and what he thought and did when he found out that he had it.

Candido was rich: with what his father had left him as well as his mother's dowry, which, in the arrangement following the annulment of the marriage, had passed to him by a gracious act of donation. Of this wealth the general was legal guardian. Candido's guardian in the official designation; the guardian of Candido's property, to all intents and purposes. Not that the general was eating into that property and its income, on the contrary he was a scrupulous administrator: but it did give him, or so he thought, a power that helped him in his political activities. It was his peasants who worked on Candido's lands, his shepherds, his cowhands. On the other hand, it must be said, he could not have robbed his grandson even if he had wanted to: Candido's father's brothers and sisters had tried to obtain the guardianship of the property, without the obligation of also being the guardians of their brother's son, who had brought about their brother's death. Having failed to obtain it, they were ever on the alert: ready to strike the general down if he was in any way lacking. They had also tried, and were still trying, to win Candido over to their side, pretending that they were intensely, painfully fond of him. The problem was that Candido, whom they, too, regarded as a monster, did not realise what they were doing – being the monster that he was. But the general also feared any possible alliance of Candido with those relatives on his father's side: which gave Candido a certain power over the general.

The threat of taking him away from his after-school classes with the archpriest Lepanto would therefore have been im-possible to realise, if Candido had genuinely objected. As he genuinely did object after the elections of 1953, when the general was again elected, but in tenth place. The reason for the fall was, according to the general, the archpriest's hostility towards him: a hostility due to Candido's having informed on him, and that unpleasant encounter he had had with the archpriest.

The knowledge that he had faded from first place in the elections of 1948 to tenth in those of 1953 had the general spitting with rage. When, on the day the results were announced, his grandson appeared, smiling as serenely as ever, he went into hysterics. He insulted him in the name of loyalty and love of family, which he himself represented, but which Candido did not know and, being the worm that he was, would never know; he insulted the archpriest in the name of other virtues such as work, chastity, fidelity and anti-Communism, virtues unknown to the archpriest. At this point, Concetta, who was present at the scene, rebelled. As far as the insults against Candido were concerned, although she disapproved, she might still agree with them: Candido was incapable of living according to the rules. But the general should not have allowed himself to utter those insults against the archpriest; especially those which cast doubts on his chastity, since everyone knew how chaste he was.

The general went and stood in front of her, pointed an accusing finger at her chest, at her conscience, and cried, 'Who did you vote for, who did that scoundrel make you vote for?' Concetta replied proudly, 'I voted for the Holy Cross, as always.' But the general insisted, 'What about my number, did you vote for it? Tell me the truth, on the souls of your departed you must tell me: did you vote for my number?' At a loss, Concetta stammered, 'That's between me and my conscience, you have no right to ask me.' 'You didn't vote for me,' the general said, painfully triumphant, 'I know it, I know it for certain.' Then, becoming indulgent and even affectionate,

'Well, I don't mind, I got elected anyway... There's just one thing I'd like to know: what did the archpriest say to stop you voting for me?' 'That's under the seal of the confessional,' Concetta replied – not realising that she herself was breaking that seal. Now the general's tone turned acid and mocking. 'The seal of the confessional! Fool, don't you realise you've just told me he was the one who told you not to vote for me? I'll tell you what's sealed...' And here he became quite obscene, alluding to Concetta's unrequited sexual feelings; unrequited even by the archpriest, despite all the love Concetta had for him.

Concetta put her hands over Candido's ears to stop him hearing his grandfather's obscenities, then hit the general where it really hurt. 'Someone who talks like that in front of a child can't be his guardian.' 'I'll talk the way I like!' the general cried angrily, then, to Candido, 'From now on, you're not going to see any more of that scoundrel.' But after Concetta and Candido had left, the woman's threatening words started to make their way in his head and calmed him down.

Meanwhile, on the way home, Concetta, in her exasperation, broke the seal of the confessional completely. She told Candido what the archpriest had told her about the voting. 'If you want to vote Christian Democrat, at least choose someone who's a little bit Christian.' Concetta had asked if the general was a little bit Christian, and the archpriest had replied, 'I wouldn't say so.' These few words had left her feeling worried, bewildered, indecisive. She had not voted for the general, although she had felt a certain remorse. Now she had purged herself of that remorse, she was sure she had done the right thing, as had the archpriest. 'He was right, oh, how right he was!' And having got that off her chest, and her hatred for the general having become as cold and hard as a diamond, she gave Candido a detailed run-through of his inheritance, revealed to him the power he had over the general, and urged him to resist and to keep going to the archpriest.

Candido did not need urging: he had already decided to continue his after-school classes with the archpriest. Now, however, he knew that he could stick to his decision, because of the power that he had, a power of which he had previously been unaware. It had never occurred to him that a man could have power over another man because of money, land, sheep, oxen – let alone that he himself might have such power. When he got home, and was alone in his room, he wept: he did not know whether it was with joy or anguish. Then he went to the archpriest and told him everything, even about the tears which had, for some reason, overcome him.

It was the first time he had stayed to have something to eat with the archpriest. And just as he had discovered that day that he was rich, so he also discovered now that the archpriest was poor.

They sat and talked until it was evening and the room grew dark and they were divided not only by the table but also by the shadows; but not really divided, since their voices had acquired a different tone, their conversation a new sense of fraternity. Wealth, poverty. Good, evil. Having power, not having power. The Fascism inside us, the Fascism outside us. 'All the things we try to fight outside us,' the archpriest said, 'are inside us; and we have first to seek them inside us and fight them... Wealth is something I desired so strongly that even my wanting to be a priest came out of that desire: the wealth of the Church, the wealth of the churches; the marble, the stucco, the gilding, the polished silver, the damask, the silk, the heavy embroidery, the threads of gold and silver... All I knew were baroque churches, baroque in everything: you enter to hear the mass, to pray, to confess; and instead you find you've entered the belly of wealth... But wealth is dead but beautiful, beautiful but dead: someone said that, though perhaps not precisely in those words. And I think that men who know something about themselves, who live and watch themselves living, can be divided into two great categories: those who know that wealth is dead but beautiful, and those who know that wealth is beautiful but dead. Everything is in the turning of those two words around the "but"… For me it is still beautiful but even more dead, even more death. But the problem is that we can never get to a point at which this death no longer tempts us, a point at which we can separate the beauty from the death… Perhaps there isn't such a point, but we have to look for it.' This speech was somewhat mysterious to Candido; but mysterious in a way that had to do with the truth, a truth that hung there so luminously that he was sure it would dissolve if, for example, he had attempted to ask what a baroque church was.

The archpriest had changed a lot in the three years that Candido had been going to see him. The general was hurt that he had discouraged the female penitents from voting for him; many others were hurt that he hadn't paid the same attention to the elections as he had in 1948, that he had in fact sown doubt and uncertainty among the Catholics. What was worse, he continued to marry Communists in church, to baptise their children, to tolerate red flags at funerals, despite the fact that the Communists were to be considered excommunicate. Yes, he had changed a lot: to the extent that it no longer bothered him whether or not his treatise on moral psychology received the bishop's *imprimatur*. Candido was aware of the change: he saw him becoming less active, more tired, more absorbed, more indifferent. But he did not realise that this change was partly due to him, to the new sense of responsibility which the archpriest, for himself and for him, had slowly, all unnoticed, begun to assume towards life: a different sense of responsibility from what he had previously felt in his ministry. More human, more direct, more anxious and constant.

That evening, however, the hard-won decision they both came to was this: that, although there was no way to prevent the general from fearing that Candido would change sides and turn to his relatives on his father's side for better guardianship, even making use of the archpriest's protection and Concetta's now fierce animosity towards the general, Candido would do nothing, make no threats, to foster such a fear in his grandfather. A hypocritical decision – the archpriest commented – but one which reduced to the minimum the curse of power for someone like Candido who now knew he had it.

How Candido and the archpriest
found themselves discovering the perpetrator
of a mysterious crime; and how both
were condemned by the whole town, and
the archpriest also by the hierarchy.

A parish priest at the newest church in the newest neighbour-hood in town had been murdered: in the sacristy, soon after the bells of that church had rung out the Ave Maria. The murderer's identity was unknown, and neither theft nor revenge seemed to be the motive. There was nothing, or very little, to steal in the church; and nothing was missing. And the priest, apart from the usual involvement in the elections, did not seem to have done anything that might lead someone to kill him. The police and the Carabinieri were floundering. The bishop wrote the arch-priest a heartbroken letter, hoping that such a terrible crime, committed against a priest of the Church of Christ, would not remain unpunished.

A police superintendent came from the provincial capital; and before beginning his investigation he decided to speak to the archpriest about the case. Candido was in the archpriest's quar-ters when the superintendent arrived. The superintendent tried, more than once, to get the archpriest to make Candido leave. But the archpriest had thought it might be a good idea to see how Candido reacted to the interview, and if it reminded him of another many years earlier. If there was some dark thing that had set hard inside Candido, this might be the moment for him to break free of it. He urged the superintendent to speak freely, as if Candido was not there: in any case, he could be sure that the boy would not reveal a single word of their conversation outside that room. Not convinced, in fact somewhat uneasy, the superintendent nevertheless began to recount everything he knew so far: the official reports, the results of the post mortem.

The parish priest had been killed soon after the sacristan had rung the Ave Maria: an important detail because, once he had rung it, the sacristan tried to enter the sacristy to tell the priest that he needed to pop home for a short time: but the door, unusually, was locked from the inside. The priest was talking to someone in there. The sacristan knocked. 'What do you want?' the priest asked, and the sacristan replied, 'Nothing, I just wanted to tell you that I have to go home for something,' and the priest said, 'All right, but don't be long.' And he went back to talking with whoever it was.

The sacristan confessed that he had stood there for a while, eavesdropping. He heard the other man speak, and recognised the voice of a lawyer named... 'I won't tell you the name,' the superintendent said, 'because it's not right to involve him in this business: in fact it's been established that he has nothing to do with it.' Coming back half an hour later, the sacristan had found the door still closed. He listened for a moment, but all was silent: the lawyer must have gone. He tried the handle, and the door opened. It was so dark inside that he stumbled over the priest's corpse. He had been killed: three bullets, so well-aimed that one would have been enough, from a gun that the experts had identified as German army issue: the kind that until a few years earlier could still be found in the local markets.

The lawyer was interviewed, and calmly stated that the sacristan must have been dreaming when he heard his voice: he had been at home all that evening, busy preparing for a trial the following day. He had often been to see the priest, who was both a friend and colleague (the lawyer was advisor to the San Giovanni di Dio hospital, of which the priest was chairman): but not that evening, definitely not. Neither the Carabinieri nor the sacristan could doubt the lawyer's word. The sacristan agreed that he must have been mistaken: it was an easy mistake to make, given that the sacristy – they had tested this for themselves – had a bit of an echo, which tended to make voices sound different. 'That's all we have,' the superintendent concluded. 'In other words, nothing.'

It was at this point that Candido said, as if to himself, 'The voice.'

'What do you mean, the voice?' the superintendent said, turning to him irritably. He had foreseen that the boy might interfere: one of those tiresome, overzealous, know-it-all kids that priests like to have around.

'Voices,' Candido said calmly, 'are almost always right.'

The superintendent wavered between anger and dismay. He turned back to the archpriest, his face like a question mark: a question mark starting in his flashing left eye, curving across the lines on his forehead, thinning and darkening with doubt in his right eye as it descended, and finishing in a mouth open in indignation and amazement.

The archpriest had turned pale. He seemed to be thinner, and his forehead was gleaming with sweat. He was full of astonishment and dread: because Candido had caught what he himself had been thinking, what he himself should have said but hadn't wanted to. After a long silence he said, 'Voices are almost always right, and things are almost always simple.'

The superintendent still seemed frozen in a mute question. Then, as if coming round from a hypnotic state, the archpriest said, 'If you told me the lawyer's name, I think I would have the solution, from what you've told me, but I wouldn't like there to be any misunderstanding... Would you be so kind as to tell me?' Automatically, as if he, too, had now entered a hypnotic state, the superintendent told him the name. 'Thank you,' the archpriest said. 'Excuse me, I'll be right back.' He stood up and went into the other room. Candido guessed that he needed to collect himself, to pray. When he returned, he was calmer. He said simply, 'I'm sorry, but it's possible.'

'What is?' the superintendent asked.

'That voices are almost always right and things are almost always simple.'

Half understanding, half not wanting to understand, the superintendent stammered, 'You mean…'

'Precisely,' said the archpriest.

'But why?'

'You won't find that out from me,' the archpriest said firmly.

He did in fact find it out from others – without too much difficulty, all things considered. He found it out, last but not least, from the lawyer himself. He had gone to see the priest in a final attempt to persuade him to marry his daughter, a girl of eighteen who had been seduced by the priest and was expecting a child: but the priest had adopted such a negative, contemptuous attitude that he had fully deserved those three well-aimed bullets. More than a week had gone by, but the lawyer did not show a hint of remorse; as a lawyer, he had only one concern: finding as many witnesses as he could to say that he always had the gun with him, that he had not brought it with the premeditated intention of killing the priest. In fact, the whole town approved of him, even applauded him, for two reasons: he had avenged his honour, and he had avenged it on a priest. A sudden outburst of anticlericalism seized the region, as if a volcano so long dormant as to be thought extinct had suddenly erupted. And as everyone knew what had happened, that it had been Candido and the archpriest who had delivered the perpetrator of the crime into the hands of the police, the bishop soon found out about it, and sent a learned theologian to investigate the case. The result of this investigation was that the archpriest was asked, first in a thinly veiled way, then explicitly, to resign as an archpriest: he could not continue to hold that office if all the faithful now not only disapproved of him, but despised him. Not – said the learned theologian – that telling the truth wasn't a fine thing: but sometimes it caused so much damage that not telling it was not a sin but was actually praiseworthy.

Handing his resignation letter to the theologian, the now ex-archpriest said in a mocking, almost singsong tone, '*I am the way, the truth and the life*; but sometimes I am the dead end, the lie and the death.'

The theologian took that rather badly. But the ex-archpriest was in a mood that was close to joyful.

How the ex-archpriest attempted to devote himself to cultivating his own garden and Candido his own land; and how they both faced disappointment.

Candido did get shown a little respect by his classmates – they looked at him as if he had been an actor in a detective film – but the ex-archpriest was not shown any respect by anyone.

To the general, the whole affair, which had aroused the indignation of the whole town and had even angered the bishop to such an extent that he had demoted the archpriest Lepanto, was the last straw. He wrote to his daughter, telling her about the scandal, about the scandalous behaviour of Candido and Lepanto, and asking if now might not be the time to reconsider that old, excellent idea – he underlined the word excellent – of taking Candido to America. Maria Grazia's answer was harsh and firm. Whose bright idea had it been to entrust Candido to the archpriest Lepanto? Certainly not hers: she had always respected priests, but she didn't trust them. It was therefore up to the general to separate Candido from the ex-archpriest. As far as taking him to America, it wasn't possible: apart from the traumatic effect it might have on Candido, did he think it was possible for a thirteen-year-old boy, who had lived until then in Sicily, to come into a quiet, almost happy American family without upsetting it?

In his answer, the general threatened to renounce the guardianship of Candido; but Maria Grazia knew he would never renounce it, and she was adamant. She did, however, promise to make a flying visit to Sicily. Which she did, unexpectedly, many months later: just when Candido, in the company of the ex-archpriest of course, had left for Lourdes, as a stretcher bearer, on a train carrying the sick, the lame and the blind to a hoped-for miracle. But of that journey, which so impressed

Candido's mother when she found out about it that it made the general's judgement seem unjust and his worries exaggerated, there will be more to say later.

Meanwhile, the ex-archpriest – who from now on we shall call Don Antonio, as Candido called him – had moved from his quarters in the cathedral to the house, uninhabited for many years, which he had inherited from his father. The crucifix, the inkwell and the books were now on a small, wobbly table. The house was small and damp, but it had a kitchen garden, overrun with nettles, which Don Antonio now stubbornly set about cultivating in order to get from it the little he needed, he said, to get by. He found his father's old tools and, rusty and unsound as they were, set to work, helped sometimes by Candido. As far as seeding and transplanting, fertilising, hoeing and weeding were concerned, he trusted to his memories of what he had seen his father do all those years ago: but either because his memory failed him or because the earth and the air, the sunshine and the rainfall, the cycle of the seasons had changed, everything came up looking weak and diseased. But he did not grow discouraged: as with everything in life that bore fruit, it was, he thought, a question of love; he had not yet learnt to love the earth and the work as fully as he should.

Don Antonio's kitchen garden reminded Candido that he owned land. He went and had a look at it, and did a kind of census: how large an area it covered, how many people worked there, what crops were grown, how many sheep and oxen grazed on it. So much land, and so few people working it: they had almost all gone to Belgium, or France, or Venezuela, and the few who remained had grown melancholy, not only because of their age but because their children had left them to go to those distant countries. If their children had gone, and if it was unlikely that they would ever return, what was the point in staying and working the land?

Candido asked the general for permission to take care of his own land. The general granted it – on condition that he did not ask him for any money for tools, machines and improvements. 'If things stay as they are,' he said, 'you can still get something out of it. But if you try and do something new, your income will go, and so will the land.' Candido told him that he would not ask him for money for implements and improvements: he simply wanted to go there and work. What he did need, in order to get there and back more quickly than on a bicycle, was a motorbike. The general's response was prompt and even generous: he bought him a motorbike, one of the most powerful there was – perhaps in the hope that he would break his neck. That is our conjecture, not Candido's: Candido simply thought that such generosity on the part of his guardian was a prize for his doing well at school and for never asking him for money, apart from his small monthly allowance. In addition, Candido was a careful rider: he did not care about reaching high speeds or making a lot of noise. Calmly and regularly, he would ride out to the country, do his two or three hours of hoeing, and ride back. He had chosen for himself a piece of land close to a spring, he had turned the soil and fertilised it thoroughly; so thoroughly that what he sowed came up looking burnt. He had based his work on what he had read in a manual, what he had seen Don Antonio doing and what the peasants had advised him to do. Just following the first two would have resulted in half a failure, but taking the peasants' advice had ensured that it was a complete failure. They had never seen the general on that land; so, in a way, they respected him and were even quite fond of him. The women and some of the old men even voted for him; the others solemnly promised that they would and then swore that they had, but instead voted for the Communist Party. But Candido, who came there every day now, they hated. They thought he was there to spy on them, to harass them. It also seemed to them that the work he was doing on the land was just a hobby for him, a kind of whim, which made a mockery of their own work. Candido assumed that they were happy to see him and talk to him; just as he was happy to be with them, to listen to their opinions, their stories, their fables. He also performed little services for them, bringing them things they needed from the town. But he never succeeded in undermining their age-old hatred of the landowning class; a hatred which the general's absenteeism had attenuated somewhat over the past few years and which Candido's constant presence now revived in no uncertain terms. What was more, Candido seemed to them a kind of usurper, a thief. And not only of them and their work – a landowner was always that – but of the property of the late lamented lawyer Munafò (who had been unbearable when he was alive, but was now late and lamented because he was dead and because of the way he had died): property that Candido was in no way entitled to, if he really was the person responsible for the poor lawyer having become late and lamented.

As we have said, Candido was unaware of the peasants' hatred; but he did feel uneasy about owning the land. Why should all that land be his? How could it be that a man – his grandfather or great-grandfather – who had never done any work on it, or perhaps only a tiny amount, had made it his? And was it right to receive it, as he, Candido, had received it, and keep it for himself? These were questions he asked himself and also asked the peasants, and, hearing them, the peasants hated him all the more. But the answers they gave him were to the effect that whatever property you have, you have for the sake of your children, and it's all right for your children, and your children's children, to keep it and enjoy it and pass it on intact to your whole line of descent. And that was what they really thought; but not in relation to Candido, who had inherited his property through a legitimacy that had nothing to do with the only real legitimacy, which came from the son being so like the father as to be almost identical with him, the son living according to the father's rules and not betraying the father, whether he was right or wrong (especially, in fact, if he was wrong). Apart from that, they were sick and tired of that whole business of giving the land to the peasants, to those who worked on it: it was because of that mirage that they had followed the Communist Party, and still followed it; wearily, though, without believing in it and without wanting it. 'The land is tired,' they would say, 'and we're more tired than the land.' Candido imagined that if he yielded the land to the workers, which was what he planned to do as soon as the law allowed it, the children who had emigrated would come home and all the land that was now uncultivated and given over to grass and scrub would once again be clear, tidy and productive. But when, one day, he said this to the peasants, he was told that the children would certainly return, but only to sell the land and go back again to where they were now. They told him this with a certain scorn: for him, and for the land.

This was a disappointment to Candido. He lost his enthusiasm, and felt that there was something ridiculous in this desire of his to play the peasant. He liked the work, it made him feel healthy, gave him a healthy appetite and let him sleep healthily; but in addition to the sense of being ridiculous, he was starting to be worried by the fact that he enjoyed it as a privilege: the age-old privilege of the boss, which used to be just income, but now was the almost sporting pleasure of cultivating, however clumsily, a little kitchen garden.

He and Don Antonio talked about this at some length. Neither was prepared to accept defeat. And before defeat finally came, Don Antonio had the idea of a pilgrimage to Lourdes. 'You'll see how much good it'll do us,' he said mysteriously to Candido: as if he were talking about a detoxification cure.

How Candido and Don Antonio travelled to Lourdes; and the good it did both of them.

Don Antonio had already been to Lourdes once, in the summer of 1939, just before the outbreak of war. He had then been the age that Candido was now: so that, in going back there after nearly twenty years, it was as though he was being torn between the impressions he had had as a fifteen-year-old, which he would confirm and, in a way, relive through Candido, and those he would have now. The difference was that then he had been a seminarian full of fear and shame with regard to sin and spots which he believed were marks of sin and a devotion to the Virgin Mary in which he became absorbed to purge himself of sin; while Candido was completely impervious to the idea that there were any sins apart from lying and humiliating other people and making them suffer, and he did not feel any devotion to images of the Virgin Mary and the saints which were not well painted or sculpted – and even then it wasn't a question of devotion, but of admiration and pleasure.

Although often urged to do so by Candido, Don Antonio always refused to talk about his impressions of that first visit; but we can say that it did rather liberate him both from his obsessive preoccupation with sin and from his no less obsessive devotion to the Virgin Mary; and from it he had derived that little bit of practicality and skill that had launched him on a career – from chaplain to parish priest, from parish priest to archpriest in a short time – which had now come to an abrupt end. And this, too, we can say: Don Antonio was undertaking this new journey to Lourdes with the aim of obtaining from it a further, final liberation.

The afternoon they set off from Palermo, the sirocco was blowing hard. Thanks to the train that had brought them to Palermo having been delayed, Don Antonio and Candido arrived just as the special train for Lourdes was about to leave. The lady who seemed to be in charge of the convoy and the priest who was with her reprimanded both of them for the delay, especially Candido who, as a stretcher bearer, should have been there at least two hours earlier; but the reprimand, although harsh in its substance, was charitable and almost supplicatory in tone and choice of words. This disturbed Candido, and, had it not been for Don Antonio, he might have gone back home. He might: but the desire to make that journey – the first in his life – was like a fever inside him: anxious, visionary, slightly delirious.

He was disturbed again, walking through the first carriage: those crutches propped against the seats, those suffering faces turning to him, those sightless eyes. But this disturbance did not make him feel the slightest regret at having undertaken that journey, rather a sense of astonishment and admiration for the ability to gather and organise so much suffering into a convoy of hope. There was, in that aggregate of suffering, in that organisation and display of physical misfortune, something repugnant and at the same time a kind of grandeur. And while Candido, in that first moment, felt the grandeur, Don Antonio was visibly overcome with repugnance; a repugnance that had barely been a glimmer on his first journey, had grown in his memory and his thoughts, and was now fully confirmed. Not because of those bodies, those sores, those aqueous or blank eyes, that drooling; but because of that organised, transported hope.

In the two days it took them to reach Lourdes, Candido's astonishment and admiration gave way to repugnance. He talked of other things to Don Antonio; and Don Antonio talked of other things to him. However, after a time, Candido could not help saying, 'If I were God, I'd be offended by all this.' And Don Antonio nodded his head and smiled wearily. But, as a counterweight to the repugnance, there was in Candido – and it was also noticeable in the other stretcher bearers, the nurses, the nuns, the priests – a growing sense of physical elation, a euphoria, almost a celebration of good health, of appetites and desires. The girls and ladies of good family who were acting as nurses and who, during the early stages of the journey, seemed rigid, fixed in a voluntary state of self-mortification, just as they were in everyday life, in the life of their bodies, when night fell acquired a looseness, a devastating vitality, a flourishing, effusive carnality, which made even the ugly ones look beautiful. And the stretcher bearers and priests seemed to be having the same, or a similar, effect on the nurses and the nuns, judging by the tremulous, almost warbling tone of joyful apprehension with which they addressed one another, the luminous, vaguely ecstatic looks they exchanged. And what happened to Candido on the second night was something that had to happen, that couldn't not happen in that Manichean universe of sickness and health which the train had become. As he had on the first night, he woke as dawn was breaking and went out into the corridor. A nurse was walking past him when the train gave a sudden lurch, and Candido felt her body pressed against his, weighing on him as if the wall against which he was leaning had become a floor. Instinctively, he moved his arms to stop her from falling and hold her against him: and it was as if the train were frozen, suspended in that sudden movement. He felt himself being groped through his clothes and then avidly searched for under his clothes: and he never knew if it was a moment before or a moment later or in the same moment that he himself began to mould her body through her clothes, to grope for her, to search for her. Because of the intensity with which his hands were feeling their way, he had an abrupt image of himself as a blind man, as if that body was only clear in his mind through the indications transmitted to it by his touch. For a long time they kissed, and Candido felt and saw, saw in his deep, oh-so-sweet blindness, himself and the world become a sphere of iridescent liquid, of music.

The girl pulled free of him, and silently walked away along the half-dark corridor. She turned before she disappeared, which meant that Candido was able to recognise her the next day. She wasn't beautiful, though you wouldn't call her ugly. But as long as that journey lasted, for Candido she would be very beautiful. But in the hours that remained, and on the return journey, her eyes glided over Candido with an indifference which made him think that he might have made a mistake, that he had experienced that moment of love with someone else. Don Antonio reassured him: not because he knew the girl, but because he knew the world of Catholic charity, and those acts of fleeting love, of sin, like those flowers called *belles de nuit*, which only open at night, were part of it.

Of the journey to Lourdes, with its sadness and its badness, what Candido was left with was that joy, that revelation, that miracle. In fact, he was the only one on that train to have experienced a miracle. Don Antonio had meant it to be a way of vaccinating Candido against Catholicism; and for himself a farewell, a leave-taking. But, despite the variation that had befallen Candido, the balance sheet was still positive. Candido could now be considered both vaccinated and immune. And as for himself, he was completely cured, untethered, free.

How the love of women, and of a woman, took hold of Candido; and what Don Antonio said to him on the subject.

On returning from Lourdes, Don Antonio stopped being a priest. He wanted Candido to call him simply Antonio, but every now and again Candido let slip a *Don* (and so do we). He had become more cheerful, more light-hearted, wittier; to the point of seeming cynical and blasphemous to those who were not witty. 'I used to be cynical and blasphemous,' he would say, 'and now that I'm not, they accuse me of those vices.' And, often, he declared that he had become very religious. As evidence of this finally attained religiousness of his, he adduced the luxuriance of his kitchen garden: the earth was now aware of him as a man, and was responding to his passion. Candido was not so sure of that: the earth was responding because he had become more skilful and experienced in his work. But he could not help thinking that what Don Antonio said about the earth was true of woman, of women: on the train to Lourdes, he had discovered that love responds to love. And as he could feel that experience slipping away like a dream, becoming vaguer, more imprecise with every day that passed, he wanted to repeat it, his one thought was to repeat it, pin it down, confirm it; and complete it. He talked about this to Don Antonio, since he was accustomed to talking to him about everything, freely, without exception and without shame.

'You see,' Don Antonio would say, 'women belong to my past as a priest. To love them really, or to love one of them, I should free myself of that past. It was like a long illness, and now I am convalescing. It's easy enough to knock down all the dogmas, the simulacra and symbols which have been part of your life, one after the other, like targets in a shooting gallery: I'd say all you need is the little rifle of Voltaire's *Dictionary*, if the mist has cleared from your eyes. But all those dogmas, all those simulacra, those symbols you think you have destroyed come together again in the body of a woman, in the idea of love or simply of making love. I feel the truth is so much with me, in all things, all thoughts, that at times I have the impression that I have crossed the threshold of the secret, of the mystery: which is that there is no secret, there is no mystery; that everything is simple, both inside and outside us. But loving or making love in this simplicity, or on the verge of it, I don't think would be possible for me, nor would I like to. And however free we feel, I think that in these things the Church, the Churches, those that there are, and those still to come, will get the better of us. Between Saint Paul's epistles and Stendhal's *On Love* the argument turns on the same burning line: the hell of the other world, the hell of this one; and it's a beautiful argument.'

'But love is simple,' Candido would say.

'Not for me,' Don Antonio would say. 'The hell of love is still my paradise.'

Candido was again to experience the simplicity of love, an earthly paradise without divine prohibitions or diabolical temptations: only this time it came close to other people's hell.

We have so far neglected to mention that the general, a widower since before the war in Spain, had a woman who kept house for him, and was therefore called the housekeeper. Not always the same one: since '39 there had been four or five of them and, as he himself got older, the housekeepers got younger: the latest one to take on the job was really very young. That had been a couple of years before. Exemplary in keeping house, she was the best the general had ever had: in the opinion of the general himself, borne out by the hatred towards her that Concetta could not hide. That *that woman* (which was what Concetta called her) kept the house cleaner and tidier than she had ever known it to be, that she could cook well (which was clear from the smells wafting from the kitchen), that the general's shirts were well-ironed, was an admission it pained Concetta to make, but Concetta found some compensation in the fact – an indisputable fact, in her opinion – that *that woman* had come from one of those unmentionable houses which had been abolished by law. Nor was she in any doubt that *that woman* slept with the general. To tell the truth, no one who knew the general and had seen the housekeeper was in any doubt about that. Apart from Candido, who had never paid any attention to Concetta's insinuations. For about two years, it was as if the housekeeper had been invisible to him: one of those people who end up being relegated to the rank of objects which are there, which can't not be there, but which we are so used to seeing that we don't see them any more, and which start to exist only when they are no longer there. In addition, it seemed as if she wanted to make herself invisible: she dressed anonymously, spoke very little, and disappeared whenever the general received visitors. If anyone had asked Candido whether she was young or middle-aged, blonde or brunette, buxom or skinny, he would not have been able to say. Until that afternoon in late summer when, while he was reading Marx, he saw on the page the grey-blue eyes, a strand of blonde hair, the line of the mouth, the curve of the breasts: as if these things were sketches for a painting that had still to be completed.

He shut the book, stood up and left the house. He went straight to his grandfather's house, where he had not set foot for months, to verify and complete the image that had appeared to him. And he was so struck by that image that not even for a moment did he think about the general, or wonder whether or not he was absent (there was usually a fifty-percent likelihood that he would be, but in summer, because of the Parliamentary recess, it became twenty-five percent).

The general was in Rome, she told him as soon as Candido entered. She was a little sleepy, her hands slow and hesitant as she tied the belt of her blue dressing gown. She did not ask him what he wanted, but began walking towards the drawing room, and Candido walked behind her, letting his eyes slowly trail over her body, which showed through the thin material, and over her movements, which seemed, as she walked and at the same time raised her hands to tidy her hair, like the slow beginning of a dance.

In the almost dark drawing room, she turned to look at him: her eyes were laughing even though her mouth seemed sullen. She took a handkerchief from the pocket of her dressing gown and lightly mopped her lips and eyelids with it. It slipped from her hand, or she dropped it. It fell to the carpet. 'Candide picked it up. She innocently took his hand, and the young man innocently kissed the young girl's hand with a particular warmth, sensitivity and grace; their lips met, their eyes lit up, their knees trembled, their hands strayed.'

Unlike his namesake, whose adventures and misadventures had left Lambert's printing press two centuries earlier, Candido had his pleasure that day, fully, calmly and at length. A pleasure shared by Paola, fully, calmly and at length. Not only that day, but also in the days and months that followed; indeed, nearly a year would pass before the general, informed by an anonymous letter, caught them in the act.

How Candido and Don Antonio felt about Communism; and the discussions they had between themselves and with their comrades.

Candido, as we have said, was reading Marx. He had first read Gramsci, then Lenin, and now he was reading Marx. He was bored with Marx, but he persisted. The works of Gramsci,[4] on the other hand, he had read with great interest; he felt quite moved when he imagined that frail, sickly little man who devoured books and wrote down his reflections, and in this way had overcome prison and the Fascists who had put him there. He really felt as though he could see him, could see the cell, the table, the notebook, the hand writing, and hear the scratching of the pen on the paper. He had often talked to Don Antonio about Gramsci and what he had just read by Gramsci; but Don Antonio did not like Gramsci very much, he saw an error in the pages of the notebooks, spreading like a fault line. The Italian Catholics: where had Gramsci seen them? On Sunday, at midday mass: because apart from that they didn't exist. They were a weakness, and Gramsci had started to make them a force: in the history of Italy, in the future of the country. 'Let's hope the error doesn't develop, and the fault line doesn't grow wider,' he would say. But it seemed to Candido that Don Antonio was not exactly impartial on the subject of Catholicism. There was still too much disappointment, too much resentment in him from his days as a priest, so that what he had been had a little too much influence on what he wanted to be.

Candido had also been bored by Lenin, but in a different way from Marx, and much less so. The image he had got of Lenin was that of a carpenter who had gone to great effort to hit the same nails right at the top of a structure; but even with all that effort, some nails had gone in badly or got twisted.

He had emerged from the pages of Lenin as if leaving behind him the din of a building site; and had entered those of Marx the way you would, after visiting a building site, enter the foreman's office. And just as it isn't easy for everyone, and difficult for most people, to read the charts and blueprints hanging or lying there, so it seemed to Candido that he was wandering through the pages of Marx without being able to read them. And this impression, this unease, lasted until, after reading everything of Marx that he could get his hands on, he reread the *Communist Manifesto*. Then it became clear to him that, although there were indeed many things he may not have been able to read, there were others he had not understood for the very reason that he had understood them: that is, he had refused to believe that Marx could have wanted to say, or had said, precisely those things. When, at school, he had studied Machiavelli, he had been very struck, in the sense that he had begun to think that perhaps Machiavelli was not very intelligent, by the fact that he could have believed in a future in which firearms would be cast aside to return to cold steel. And what Marx, starting with that great, simple truth about capital, about capitalism, that great, simple discovery, then put forward seemed to him of the same order as that prediction of Machiavelli's about the return to cold steel. Was it not possible to see, even then, Candido wondered, that capitalism would have a choice, like the choice between cold steel and firearms? And how could anyone not realise that people would stick with firearms and perfect them, make them ever deadlier?

It was a thought – a suspicion and a question – that he was afraid and reluctant to express, even when he was alone with Don Antonio and they were talking, as they so often did, about being Communists, and about the texts of Communism. To Candido, being a Communist was simply a fact, like wanting a drink when you were thirsty; and he didn't care much about the texts. To Don Antonio, it was a very complicated, very subtle matter, all precisely defined in an apparatus of references to the texts and the glosses on them. Some of the things Candido blurted out he was then unable to explain even to himself, let alone demonstrate them, like theorems, to Don Antonio. As a result, whenever he felt that Don Antonio did not agree with him and demanded a demonstration, he tended to clam up as if already defeated, even though he did not feel defeated. Once, he happened to remark that, compared with Lenin and Marx, Victor Hugo and Zola and even Gorky *were better*. 'What do you mean, *better*?' Don Antonio had replied in surprise, almost in anger. '*Better* in what way?' Candido, although he knew very clearly what he felt, managed only with a great deal of difficulty and effort to say that they *were better* because they talked about things that still existed, whereas with Marx and Lenin it was as if they talked about things that had ceased to exist. 'Those writers talk about things that existed then, but it's as if they were talking about things that came later. Whereas Marx and Lenin talk about things that were still to come, and it's as if they were talking about things that no longer exist.' But this was not enough for Don Antonio, and he continued questioning him; and Candido could say nothing in reply except that if he had only read Marx and Lenin he would not be a Communist, only someone who had come to a kind of masked ball, dressed in a costume from the time of Marx, the time of Lenin. A reply which to Don Antonio seemed to indicate that Candido was very mixed up inside himself; but Candido could not say anything else to clarify to Don Antonio what he saw very clearly inside himself.

In other words, for Candido, being a Communist was almost a fact of life: capitalism was leading mankind to disintegration and extinction; Communism had grown out of the instinct for conservation, the will to survive. In other words, Communism was something to do with love, even with making love: in Paola's bed, in the general's house. Don Antonio understood this and, generally and generically, approved of it; but as far as he himself was concerned, and his own Communism, he had quite a different idea. 'A priest who is no longer a priest,' he would say, 'either marries or becomes a Communist. One way or another, he must still be on the side of hope, but in one way or another, not both.' Candido did not understand. Don Antonio would explain, 'A man who has not been a priest can have a family and be a Communist. In fact, having a family may be thought an additional reason for becoming a Communist. I say "may be thought", because actually, after a while, the family inevitably ends up leaning more towards conservatism than revolution. But a man who has been a priest and is no longer a priest because he has realised that all his ministry boiled down to was being a dead man burying other dead men, and has become a Communist, can't run the risk of ending up conservative. He might as well have stayed a priest. The celibacy the Church still imposes on priests is the only revolutionary element still left in the Church, even if now it's only paid lip service to.' Candido still did not understand. Or rather: he did not want to understand, because there were times he feared that Don Antonio was simply moving from one Church to another. And he even said as much, once: making Don Antonio very worried and anxious.

They both wanted to join the Party; but the Party, particularly in the person of Deputy Di Sales, did not seem especially well disposed to welcome them. If Don Antonio had been one of those priests who leave the Church after a long conflict with the hierarchy, and make a lot of noise about it, his admission to the Party would have been greeted as a significant event. But he had left after being demoted, and accepting his demotion in silence. And besides, he was not popular, above all because he had been responsible for the imprisonment of that poor lawyer who had redeemed his daughter's honour, his family's honour, by killing a very bad priest (in other words, as many people thought, a priest like any other priest, including Don Antonio). And as for Candido, there were a whole raft of reasons why he should not be admitted to the Party: including a mother who had run away with the American officer who had had control of the town and had favoured Fascists and Mafiosi, and the fact that he was the nephew of a Fascist general who had become a Christian Democrat deputy, and the fact that he was rich. Not as rich as Deputy Di Sales, but rich. That was why, when they applied to join the Party, he prevaricated for a long time; and they were accepted only when the Party (that is, Deputy Di Sales) realised that many young Communists, students and artisans were starting to form a circle around Don Antonio and Candido.

Almost every evening, these young people gathered in Don Antonio's house. It had all started one evening when Candido had brought a school friend, his only school friend, with him to Don Antonio's house: a poor, intelligent boy, and a Communist. And that was the first link in a chain of friendship and solidarity, which Don Antonio was able to cultivate and develop with spontaneity of heart as well as the skill of an ex-archpriest. To make a living, Don Antonio gave private lessons, helping with their graduation theses (in Italian literature, Latin literature and philosophy) those young people who had no idea about writing a thesis. In the evening he held those discussions with the young Communists, which were a kind of school. Deputy Di Sales found this a worrying phenomenon; and at the same time, these young people were putting pressure on him to admit Don Antonio and Candido to the Party. He therefore decided to admit them, but gave those he most trusted the task of keeping an eye on the two of them and denouncing them at the slightest sign of unorthodoxy. He asked Don Antonio to move those evening meetings from his house to the Party offices; so that the Party offices became a kind of evening school, quite free and unstructured, different every evening, where they talked about Marxism and psychoanalysis and the national and international situation.

But it couldn't last. And in fact it didn't.

How everyone was angry with
Candido and Paola; and how Paola moved
to Candido's house and Concetta left.

An anonymous letter, as we have said, informed the general that his housekeeper and his nephew were 'lying together' in his absence. These were the exact words used: and if the general had reflected for a moment, he would have been able, as would almost everyone in town if they had seen it, to recognise the writer of the letter: the municipal clerk Scalabrino, an assiduous reader of Boccaccio and a no less assiduous and always anonymous certifier of sexual and administrative offences. But as soon as he had read it, the general was in no fit state to reflect: torn in his pride between the desire not to believe or to ignore and the will to know. The latter prevailed, to his detriment: and he surprised Candido and Paola as they were 'lying together'. He called Candido a scoundrel and Paola a slut, screamed that he would kill them, and ran out of the room, still screaming, saying they deserved to die and would die. Paola and Candido thought that he had run to fetch a rifle or pistol from his collection and would soon reappear and shoot them dead. But they had time to dress, and still the general had not reappeared. Nor could they hear him. They were seized with a fear that was greater than the fear of seeing him come back armed. Silently, cautiously, they started looking for him.

The general was in the drawing room, sitting motionless in an armchair as if he had fallen into it, a lifeless look in his eyes. Without moving, he said, 'Out, get out of here now. I never want to see the two of you again.' Candido felt hurt by this, Paola rather less so. They left, Paola just as she was, in her dressing gown. If Scalabrino had been lurking in the vicinity of the general's house, he would have had the satisfaction of registering the effect of his letter. But even though Scalabrino was not there, even though the streets seemed deserted at that hour, there were many unseen witnesses of that departure. And of the other, reverse departure, too: Concetta's departure from Candido's house, an hour later. Because when she saw Candido and *that woman* appear, both of them pale and *that woman* – now *this woman* – in her dressing gown, Concetta had first a vague intuition, then confirmation, of what had happened. When Candido said bluntly that Paola had come to stay with them, Concetta let out a heartrending cry, crossed herself, and still yelling said that she couldn't stay anywhere *this woman* was: and she pulled her things out of the wardrobes, quickly bundled them up, and carried them downstairs and across the hall to the front door, loudly cursing *this woman*, and Candido, and the ex-archpriest: lost souls, all three of them. And she went straight to the general's house, as if it were the most correct, most obvious thing for her to go there and for the general to welcome her. For hours they did not speak; until the general suggested she sleep in the room that had been *that woman's*, and Concetta refused contemptuously, saying she preferred the tiniest cubby-hole to that comfortable room, now irredeemably tainted by the sin of *that woman*: and that opened the flood-gates to the ferment of emotions inside her. Hatred for *that woman* and for the ex-archpriest, both equally condemned to eternal damnation, the latter for tempting and corrupting Candido's mind and the former his body; remorse towards the general, because she had not voted for him and had not trusted him when he had said that the then archpriest was already a scoundrel, even before he was demoted and stopped being a priest; pity for Candido, who was ruined now, and lost; and commiseration for herself and for the general, both shamefully betrayed by those two beings now fallen into the abyss of bestiality (although in Candido's case, it was all *that woman's* fault). Yes, both of them had been betrayed – to be fair, the general deservedly, herself undeservedly. 'How could a man like you take a woman like that into his house?' The general made a gesture in reaction to this, but it was a weary one. 'Let's not start on that. Don't you think I blame myself? That should be enough. Go and sleep, now.'

'Sleep?' Concetta cried in surprise. 'How can we sleep, when such things happen?... No, we have to talk. We have to talk until tomorrow.' And indeed they talked until dawn. So it was that the general's new life began.

As for Candido, the fact that he felt hurt for the general and, more sharply, for Concetta, did not stop him making love to Paola, who was dazed with happiness and freedom. Until dawn.

How Candido received admonishments
from the Party; and how they began
to prepare a case against him.

For a long time, the town buzzed with that day's events, all the comings and goings between the general's house and Candido's. The facts were duly absorbed, spiced up and malevolently embellished. It was said that the general had had a heart attack – although others said it was a stroke – that Paola was expecting a baby and no one knew whether the father was Candido or the general, and that the Christian Democrats had asked the general to resign from Parliament and the Communist Party had asked Candido to resign from the youth federation. And it was also said that Paola, as well as being the general's mistress and Candido's mistress, had also been Don Antonio's: which brought to three the number of fathers of the child she was expecting and meant that, after it was born, there would be a delightful game, the result of which would be decided by public vote, on the basis of resemblance, to establish its paternity.

Apart from the fact that Paola had left the general's house and had entered Candido's, the rest was pure imagination. There was a little truth in what was said about the Communist Party: that it was worried about the way Candido had scandalised the whole town. The same scandal, in fact, allowed the Christian Democrats to get rid of the general in the most painless and aseptic way possible. They had already tried to get rid of him at the last elections, by doing nothing to get him elected: but there had been an unexpected flood of votes for him; perhaps due to the unforeseeable fact that the electorate continued to appreciate honesty. The general was an idiot, but honest; some people said he was an idiot because he was honest – the very people in the Party who wanted to rid themselves of his presence.

The Communist Party, then, was really worried. The young people who had supported Candido and Don Antonio in their application to join the Party were summoned one by one and severely reprimanded. Then Don Antonio was summoned. Then Candido was summoned. As accused men, to defend themselves: since it was a kind of trial that the Party had initiated.

Don Antonio was faced with two charges: that he had not dissuaded Candido from that terrible affair, that relationship which was so indecent as to verge on incest (and could have done, given the influence he was known to have over Candido); and that he himself was that woman's lover, according to the rumours circulating in the town. This second accusation really upset him: he was so choked with indignation he almost felt nauseous, and at the same time, he had a sense of pity for those who had spread these rumours and those who were bringing him to account for them. If he could have had a moment to himself, he would have prayed: because he still believed in God, and still prayed. In front of the judges, he stammered: in other words, he behaved, in their eyes, like a guilty man. As for the first accusation, he said he could not distinguish between an affair and true love, unless one was prepared to give the name *affair* to what nobody had originally been scandalised by, what they had seen only as a subject for gleeful gossip: an old man getting himself a young woman in return for wages. But that a young woman and a young man should then be attracted to each other, love each other and make love, was in the natural order of things; and besides, it was no one's business but their own, no one else had the right to interfere or to censure it. An argument ensued, which the judges cut short after a while by stating, in the most unmistakable way possible, that the Party had every right to interfere when a member's private conduct gave rise to slanderous gossip, however unfounded; let alone when it was perfectly well founded, as it was in the case of Candido.

When it was Candido's turn to be interrogated and to defend himself, Candido said that it had never occurred to him that Paola had been anything more to his grandfather than a housekeeper; nor, now that they were trying to insinuate that she had been his mistress, did it enter his mind to ask her. It was something that belonged to her, to her past; whether it had been a question of love or a matter for shame; and if it had been a matter for shame, that was all the more reason why it was his duty to help her forget it and not question her about it.

They asked him if he was prepared to leave *that woman* (to them, as to Concetta, she was *that woman*) and he replied, definitely not. They asked him to reconsider, they admonished him to behave like a person awaiting a verdict: depending on his behaviour from that moment on, the verdict might be one of absolution or of condemnation. Candido felt like answering that he didn't give a damn; but he held back, hoping that it would be they, the judges, who would reconsider. Besides, it was at this time that, according to the law, he came of age; so that, from now on, he did not have to account to anyone for his own life.

How Candido divided his life between house, countryside and Party; and how he received a proposition which he did not accept.

Candido had decided to stop studying: not that he had ever really done so. Although he had done very well at school, as far as exams and marks were concerned, the one good thing about school was that it had given him the opportunity to read all those books that had nothing to do with school and a lot to do with life. Now he wanted to devote himself entirely to the land. Thanks to the general's scrupulous administration, he found himself with money in the bank. He bought tractors, which he learned to drive; he had pipes and troughs built to make proper use of the water which had previously been wasted; he put in vineyards, and greenhouses for the vegetables. He lived the life of a peasant, and at the same time that of a mechanic: he ploughed, planted, grafted, and also took care of the machines, repairing them when they broke down. Every evening, at dusk, he would return home content. And he would find Paola content. On Saturday evenings, or when there was a meeting, he went to the Party offices: not every evening, as he had done when he was still at school. He participated in the discussions, either to lead them back to the starting point, when they had strayed so far from that point that everyone had lost sight of it, or to give his own opinion in the briefest and most succinct way possible. Those few peasants who were there, especially when the talk was of agriculture, always agreed with what he said; but those who sat behind the table, beneath the portraits of Marx, Lenin and Togliatti,[5] almost never agreed. Every time they disagreed with him, Candido returned home doubting himself and his ability to see things in the correct light, and feeling sorry that he had spoken. His only small comfort was the fact that the peasants had agreed with him. That was what he liked about the Party: being in the company of peasants, artisans, miners; real, solid people, who talked about their own needs and the needs of the town in few, but specific, words; sometimes summing up a whole discussion with one proverb. And there was quite a distinct contrast, although it went unnoticed, between those who made up the membership of the Party, who by their numbers, their needs and their hopes *were* the Party, and those who represented and directed the Party: the latter's arguments were endless and elusive; whereas the former's were rapid and sharp, like shots hitting a target, and not devoid at times of a certain coarse irony. Don Antonio saw in that contrast, which no one ever pointed out as a contrast, an echo of what had always happened and was still happening in the Church: those same people who preferred not to talk too much, whose family life and social life contained more silences than words, liked long sermons and preachers who were hard to understand. 'My soul understands it,' he had once heard an old woman say of a verbose and incomprehensible preacher. The leaders of the Party still spoke to the souls of those who could themselves only speak about bodies.

And so Candido's life went on, in this fairly untroubled way, with the only black spot being the verdict which the Party had still to pronounce on his conduct, until he suddenly found himself involved in a matter which increased many people's lack of respect for him and made it likely that the verdict would incline more towards condemnation than absolution or leniency.

Quite late one evening, he received a visit from a man named Zucco, a person whose activities were not easy to define, something between a property broker and a broker of votes. Candido knew him vaguely: he had met him a few times, an attentive helper to his grandfather. In fact, he assumed that his grandfather had sent him: unaware of the fact that for some time now Zucco, having smelt the odour of death emanating from the general where politics was concerned, had not only stopped helping him, but was carefully avoiding him altogether. In fact he had something quite different to talk to Candido about. Approaching the subject in a roundabout way, almost as if he had come to compliment Candido on having fixed things with Paola and having fixed things on his property, he asked him what his intentions were concerning that piece of land just outside town which Candido perhaps did not remember he had, if he had not yet set about fixing it (the verb *fix* was a favourite of Zucco's). Candido replied that he did remember he had it, and that he might fix it up as a vineyard. Zucco's reaction was one of shock. 'That land, a vineyard? A piece of land located just outside town? But that land is worth its weight in gold, that land *is* gold!' And he explained how it was gold; that is, how it could become gold.

There was a project to build a large hospital for the town. That land was the ideal place to build it. Only if Candido had no objection. Candido replied that, of course, he had no objection to a hospital: and besides, whether he liked it or not, the town or the province or the State could simply expropriate that land, given that it would be for public use. 'Yes, of course,' Zucco said, 'but the problem is money.'

'I understand,' Candido said, although he hadn't. 'But I can give it as gift. That's obviously what I should do: we really need a hospital.'

'As a gift?' Zucco gasped in astonishment.

'Yes,' Candido said, 'I think that's possible. A donation, or whatever you call it...'

'We haven't understood one another,' Zucco said.

'Then let's try to understand one another,' Candido said.

'Well... I... I mean... The thing is...' Zucco was having great difficulty finding the right words to say to someone as naive and stupid as young Munafò. His late father would have understood immediately. So would his grandfather, even though he wasn't very intelligent, and even though he was honest (Zucco gave a grimace of disgust at the thought of the general's honesty). But who was this one like, whose son was he?

There was a dramatic silence from Zucco, and a silence of expectation and curiosity and a touch of mistrust from Candido.

'The hospital,' Zucco said at last, 'could be built on your land, or it could be built on someone else's land just outside town. Since the expropriated land will sell for a very high price, it's obvious that whoever decides where the hospital will be built will be doing a great favour to the owner of that land. And what will the owner do: won't he show his gratitude? Won't he reciprocate?'

'What do you mean, show his gratitude?' Candido asked. 'What do you mean, reciprocate?' He was starting to understand, he had assumed the attitude of a sleepy cat behind which he always hid the fact that he was paying attention.

'Show his gratitude, yes, reciprocate, by giving him a percentage of the price he'll get… I think thirty per cent would be quite reasonable, considering that whoever gets this thirty per cent will do what he can to see that the highest possible price is paid for the land.'

'And who will get this thirty per cent?'

'As far as you're concerned, only me… But there's more than one person involved… Many people, you understand…'

'No, I don't understand,' Candido said, standing up. Zucco also stood up. They looked each other in the eyes.

'Signor Zucco, I'm giving that land as a gift,' Candido said. 'And since, now that I think about it, it is the best land on which to build a hospital, if any other site is chosen I'll know why, and I'll make the whole thing public.'

'What? You're not only throwing away a piece of luck like that, but you also want to betray me for bringing it to you?' And, sadly, he added, 'Well, I should have expected it.'

'Yes, you should have expected it,' Candido said.

The next day he went to the town hall to see the mayor, taking with him a document he had written, offering to donate that land for free. The mayor thanked him, and said that the generous offer would be carefully examined; obviously there was no certainty it would be accepted: the decision would be made by a technical commission, after due deliberation...

Candido told the whole story at the next Party meeting. He was given cautious approval by those behind the table, and was assured that the Party would keep an eye on how things went. A peasant stood up and asked how they could have dared make such a proposition to a Communist, knowing that Candido was a Communist. 'Ten years ago,' he concluded, 'no one would have been unwise enough to say something like that to a Communist.' Ten years earlier, Stalin had been alive: that was what the peasant was thinking, and everyone, knowing him, knew that he was thinking that. Some laughed, others reprimanded him. The question made a big impression on Candido.

A month later, Candido found out that another piece of land had been chosen for the hospital. He again brought up the matter at a Party meeting, but in a tone that did not please those who were behind the table. An accusing tone, they said, which they did not deserve and would not tolerate. They had done what they could to make sure that Candido's offer was accepted: but technical objections had been raised, objections that appeared incontrovertible. Of course, they could appeal to other, better, less biased technicians: but that would mean that everything would grind to a halt, and who knew how long it would be before the town got its hospital? 'Do we want a scandal or a hospital?' the gathering was asked. Most wanted the hospital, Candido and a few others the hospital and the scandal. The secretary stood up and made a speech about the situation in the region, the vision the Party had for it, and the way in which the Party dealt with opposition and criticism. Every now and again, he would make a clever dig at Candido: his exhibitionism, his pride, his behaviour, the way he disregarded the Party's warnings.

Every time the secretary made one of these more or less direct references, everyone would look at Candido, but Candido stayed calm. When the secretary finished speaking, everyone seemed to be expecting Candido to say something, but all he said was, 'Comrade, you sound like Foma Fomich.' Because that was indeed the one thing he had been thinking as he listened to the secretary.

'Like who?' the secretary asked.

'Like Foma Fomich.'

'Ah,' the secretary said, as if he knew who Foma Fomich was. In fact, he would spend the next two days racking his brains over that name.

How the Party conducted a thorough investigation to identify Foma Fomich; and the opinions Candido and Don Antonio held about this character.

Foma Fomich. 'An unknown! Who was he?... An unknown! I'm sure I've read or heard that name somewhere; it must be...' (*The Betrothed*, Chapter VIII). It must, according to the secretary, be someone who had something to do with the history of the Party in the Soviet Union: it was certainly Russian. Foma Fomich. A theoretician or a policeman? 'You sound like Foma Fomich.' It was obvious that, in uttering that sentence, that name, Candido Munafò had been trying to insult him. Foma Fomich must be someone from the time of Stalin, the time of Beria.

The secretary took all the histories of the Party of the Soviet Union he could get hold of, and in each of them checked in the index for the name Foma Fomich. It wasn't there. He looked in the index to Gramsci's notebooks, looked in every book about Communism that had an index. In vain. He thought of Czechoslovakia and what had happened after the Prague Spring: but there was no name in the reports from that time that was even slightly like Foma Fomich. He phoned Deputy Di Sales, a man of formidable culture, who was always very well informed. He had heard or read that name somewhere, said the deputy: but he couldn't say where or when, he just couldn't remember. Then he phoned the regional federation and spoke to the comrade who dealt with cultural affairs and who had been in Russia many times. The comrade who dealt with cultural affairs wanted to know the context in which the name had been brought up. The secretary told him the whole story. 'Well, it's certainly Russian. I can even tell you it means Thomas son of Thomas... I'll see what I can find out...' The name went back and forth down the phone lines, reaching Party functionaries who had spent holidays in

Russia and deputies who had lived there a long time as exiles. All of them thought they had heard or read that name: but they couldn't remember when, and they couldn't remember where. It next went to the history lecturers, the historians: they were very certain they had never heard or read it. Finally, after two days, a professor of Slavonic literature solved the mystery: Dostoevsky, *The Village of Stepanchikovo,* a humorous novel from 1859. Was there an Italian translation? Yes, there was, replied the professor, when he was called again: published in Turin in 1927. The secretary begged to be sent a copy: he needed it, he said, to support his motion to expel that son of a bitch from the Party for making so many people waste so much time over Foma Fomich. The regional federation found him a copy. The secretary read it, and grew angry. A humorous novel, a comic character: that fellow Munafò would have to pay for this.

Even people outside the Party heard about this feverish search; and then, in the meeting summoned to expel Candido from the Party, the secretary spoke at length about the character, saying that he did not recognise himself in the character, and that a Communist who saw the secretary of the branch to which he belonged as a Foma Fomich was certainly unworthy of being a Communist. The result of all this was that the nickname Foma Fomich stuck to the secretary; and today, his career having advanced, even comrades from other areas know him by that name.

While everyone in the Party was doggedly, efficiently, chasing after that name, Candido and Don Antonio talked a lot about the character. What emerged from their discussions was this: Candido really did think that the organisation of this great Party, from which they were certainly about to expel him, had been handed over to a lot of Foma Fomiches, a character he saw in the same negative light – a shiftless and shifty scholar, a Tartuffe – in which Dostoevsky had seen him; while Don

Antonio, although agreeing that there were a good many Foma Fomiches among the Party cadres, did not see the character and those who resembled him in that negative light: Dostoevsky, said Don Antonio, had, *malgré lui*, given the character a degree of positivity, of positive efficiency, of positive action; and he adduced as an example the scene in which he managed to get the colonel to call him 'excellency', even though he was not en-titled to it. And yes, it was a disturbing novel, despite the label 'humorous' which the author had given it: in the sense that it could also be taken as a prefiguration and premonition of the destiny of the Communist Party, Communist parties, the Communist world; but if you wanted to take it in that way, then you had to be consistent, just as the novel itself was, and recognise that in the end Foma makes everyone happy. 'Yes,' Candido said, 'but everyone could have been happier earlier without Foma.' Don Antonio did not agree: the happiness you attain earlier with ease is not the same as the happiness you attain later with difficulty; if you are happy unconsciously, without having suffered to achieve it, you can't really call it happiness. Candido objected that such an aphorism had nothing do with Marxism, and Don Antonio admitted that it had nothing to do with Marxism, it had to do with life, with mankind. Returning to the subject of Foma, he said that what you could see in the character – in the taboos, fears and self-criticism the character arouses in the people of Stepanchikovo – was, rather, a prefiguration of Stalin and Stalinism. But Candido did not completely agree: not of Stalin, but of Stalinism after Stalin, the Stalinism of the de-Stalinisation period. In this aspect, the analogy between the novel and historical reality was specific and incontrovertible: de-Stalinisation had come from those who had so feared Stalin as to amuse him, from those whom Stalin had reduced to the status of buffoons; just as Foma Fomich, as Dostoevsky tells us before introducing the character, was a little despot who had previously seemed merely a buffoon to the late General Krachotkin.

'You're a Stalinist,' Don Antonio said. And, as Candido was about to protest, he went on, 'No, I'm not accusing you: after Bonaparte, it was those who had never been and never would be Bonapartists who were Bonapartists, that is the best, the young... You won't admit that Stalin and Foma Fomich can be compared: and yet the difference between them is only quantitative, and in a way literary: Stalin had so many more victims, real victims; whereas Foma's victims did not suffer for long and were destined for a happy ending. Tragedy and comedy.... But look, Stalin was to Marxism what Arnobius[6] was to Christianity. In both of them, an utter contempt for man, for mankind: a huge pessimism. Arnobius believed that salvation could only come from Grace, as man did not naturally have the strength to attain good. And Stalin too: except that Stalin's Grace was the police: a Grace that was manifested, we might say, through exclusion, while Arnobius' Grace was manifested through inclusion... Stalin's Grace pardoned those it didn't touch... I should point out there's a reason I'm thinking of Arnobius... Do you know who wrote the liveliest, I'd even say the most moving thing, about his seven books of *Adversus nationes*? Concetto Marchesi, the most tireless, or at least the most open, Stalinist our Party tolerated after Khrushchev's report.'

'Our Party,' echoed Candido, with bitter irony. 'You might as well say "my Party". They're sure to expel me.'

'Yes, my Party... Because, you see, I have to stay in it: leaving the priesthood twice in a few years would be a bit too much.'

'I know...' Candido said. 'But let's get back to Stalinism: it's a subject that interests me.'

'Let's get back to it,' Don Antonio said, adding ambiguously, 'We'll always get back to it.'

How Paola disappeared;
and what she forgot to take with her.

Candido was expelled from the Party. The vote was almost unanimous: only Don Antonio did not raise his hand. It was not only because he knew and liked Candido that he did not raise his hand, but because that method of voting against someone was very much like throwing a stone at him, which was why he would never raise his hand. When he told this to the people behind the table who had looked at him when the moment came to vote, he met with an indulgent smile and the quip that the Gospel was one thing and the Party another.

Candido did not take it too amiss. He maintained that he was a Communist without a party, whereas Don Antonio maintained that it was impossible to be a Communist outside the Party. And of course he did miss it, was already missing it. But he still had Paola, Don Antonio's friendship, his work on the land, his books. Paola, though, seemed to take the expulsion harder than Candido himself. She felt as if it was her fault. The more Candido tried to tell her that he really didn't care if he was in the Party or not, the more she fretted, and the unhappier with herself she appeared to be. She became gloomy, almost surly. Surly with Candido, telling him that she had led him to that first little ruin, and others might well follow. Imagining ruins in this way, she ended up creating the conditions for them to happen.

Returning from the country one day, a couple of months after his expulsion, Candido did not find Paola at home. What he found instead was a letter on the kitchen table: 'Dear Candido, I'm leaving. I don't want to cause you any more harm: it is better to lose a woman like me than to find her. I love you very much. Paola.'

There was a postscript: 'I'm taking a few things with me I know you don't care about: they'll help me to face a life which, without you, will be difficult and very unhappy.'

Candido wept. He wept all night, he wept the next day and the days after that, shut up in his house, going round and round in circles, remembering her, touching the things she had touched every day. He would drink coffee, weep, and at times fall into a sleep that was not sleep, a painful, delirious daze. On the third or fourth day – he had lost track of time – Don Antonio came, worried because he had not seen him. Candido showed him the letter, without saying a word, weeping.

Don Antonio embraced him. He could find no words to ease that pain. The first he did find were these: 'But what did she take with her?' Candido made a gesture with his hand, a gesture which meant *I don't know and don't care*, and also a gesture of impatience at that petty question. Don Antonio was mortified. 'When you've experienced poverty as a child,' he said, 'even if after that you choose it, clamour for it, make it a reason to be happy, when you least expect it or want it to it comes out in meanness and wickedness... I'm being mean and wicked right now, in wanting the person who is making you suffer to appear mean and wicked.... Or perhaps I want to find out what she took with her to help you suffer less... I don't know, I'm floundering inside too... But the fact is, I do want to know: what did she take with her?'

Candido would have liked to reply that she had taken every-thing with her, including his life. He was about to say that. But he felt ashamed, as if it were a lie: because in a part of himself, tiny and dark at the moment compared with the vast, harsh light of his pain, he could still feel his love of life, like something strong and tenacious taking root beneath that field of pain, ready to spread. In a sudden flash he even doubted his own pain: as if it were a fiction, intense enough that you could identify with it but nevertheless pure fiction – identify with a person who existed, innumerably and identically.

'What did she take with her?' Don Antonio asked again.

Candido began opening doors and drawers: rapidly, mechanically, looking almost without seeing. Then he sat down again in the armchair where he had been sitting for three or four days. Guessing rather than knowing, despite the search he had just made, and to satisfy Don Antonio's curiosity, he said, 'She took money, a little gold, maybe some silverware, too.' He was staring at a point behind Don Antonio's back: for so long and with such an indecipherable expression that Don Antonio turned to look. There was a console table there, with two silver candlesticks on it.

'The candlesticks,' Candido said. 'She forgot the candlesticks. They're very old. They may be worth more than what she took... I'll make sure she gets them.'

My God, thought Don Antonio, how false true things are! We're with Bishop Myriel, and Jean Valjean, we're in *Les Misérables*. Or is our life all the things that have ever been written?... We think we're alive, we're real, and we're nothing but the projection, the shadow of things that have already been written.

Don Antonio's thoughts reached Candido, and the memory of those pages he had read not so many years earlier unfolded before him.

'I'm playing a part,' he said. 'Or perhaps I'm starting to feel contempt for her. The thought of letting her have the candlesticks came to me, I now know, somewhere between fiction and contempt. There was no love in that thought. Even at the time I read *Les Misérables*, I thought that Bishop Myriel went beyond love, that his love spilled over into contempt... You knew very well what you wanted when you asked me what she took with her: you wanted to impoverish me. Well, here you are: I'm impoverished. Are you happy?'

'No, I'm not happy. I'm the one who's poor, really… And I want to say something to you that may increase your suffering: I'm convinced that she took with her what she did only to destroy her image in your eyes, to make you despise her…'

'We're at a melodrama,' Candido said. Then, after a long silence, he said wearily, 'But things are always simple.' He closed his eyes. After a while, Don Antonio realised that he had fallen into a deep sleep, without breathing.

When he opened his eyes again, he thought he would see Don Antonio there in front of him, and he would have to explain to him why things are always simple and why what had happened to him was simple: but hours had gone by, and Don Antonio had left.

He felt hungry. The hunger caught fire in his imagination: freshly baked bread, spaghetti odorous with oil and basil, sausages dripping with fat over the flames.

He found some stale bread and butter, and started to chew it slowly. The pain was now a quiet ghost: as if it had left him and was hiding in the darkness and silence of the house.

Candido talked to the ghost, to Paola, to Don Antonio, to the Party secretary, to the universe. He really talked; and listened to himself talking, as if he had been split in two. It was like a delirium: but what it looked like was one of those ancient ruins in which none of the pieces is missing and you just have to lift them one by one and put them together. A task to which we are poorly suited, not loving any kind of ruin. And all we can say is this: that from the fragments of his relationship with Paola, which Candido talked about, and told himself, there remained a feeling of joy, of happiness, which the end of it – Paola's leaving, and the way she had left – could not disturb or cloud. It did not matter whether Paola had left to sacrifice her love for his sake or to free herself. The fact was that she had gone: and only the facts count, only the facts have to count. We are what we do.

Intentions, especially if they are good, and remorse, especially if warranted, are things each person can risk all on, inside himself, until he falls apart or goes mad. But a fact is a fact: it does not have contradictions, it does not have ambiguities, it does not contain the different and the contrary. That Paola had gone meant only one thing to him: that something had happened between them which had shattered the harmony of their life together, the joy of their bodies. A fact. To ask questions, to investigate, to pursue it any further, would do nothing except complicate in a painful way everything that had been simple and true. They had met in the truth of their bodies, and in that joyful truth they had been together. Then, perhaps, Paola's body had yielded to her soul. To her immortal soul, her sentimental soul, her beautiful soul: and suddenly the joyful truth of her body had grown dim and distorted in her eyes; it had become an inferior possession. Temptation, lies: just like in the book of Genesis. Except that the temptation had been her soul: her immortal, sentimental, beautiful soul. It is the soul that lies, not the body. 'Our body is like a good dog leading the blind.' And with this thought, which had come to him, distinct and consolatory, amid all his other fused and confused thoughts, just as thoughts that have already been thought by others are always distinct and consolatory when our own waver, Candido again fell into a deep sleep.

How Candido decided to free himself
of his lands and to travel; and how
his relatives did their best to free him.

Without Paola, time, for Candido, was as firm and hard as
a rock, as if it had contracted and become fixed in the present:
and if you tried to turn it over, all you saw would be the past.
There was his work, there were his books, there were his
conversations with Don Antonio: but everything was repetition,
boredom, sorrow.

Candido decided that he had to make something of himself,
of his life: to stir himself in order to try and stir, inside himself,
the love of life which he felt he had not lost.

He spoke about it first to Don Antonio, who agreed. Then
he went to talk to the Party secretary – the same secretary
who had expelled him from the Party. He told him that he had
made up his mind to give his lands to the Party, to a cooperative
of peasants and technicians that was being formed inside the
Party. He did not know how exactly, what the procedure was,
what would have to be done legally; but the Party could see
to that, since they had set up a large number of cooperatives, in
Northern Italy.

The secretary listened to him with a frozen sneer. Then he
said, 'Who do you think you are, Tolstoy?' It was his most
direct way of taking revenge on Dostoevsky, to whom Candido
had turned at the Party meeting in order, as he saw it, to mock
him, and on the mysterious Foma Fomich evoked by Candido, a
name that – as he now knew – he was stuck with as a nickname.

Candido had not been expecting such a crack. Not feeling
the slightest resentment towards the secretary, he could never
have imagined that the secretary felt any towards him. He went
red, as if feeling he was to blame. But the secretary, believing he
had struck home in such a way that Candido would hate him

even more than he assumed he already did after his expulsion, became even more logically aggressive. 'Firstly,' he said, 'where am I going to find the peasants to form a cooperative? The few that are left prefer to work by the day on other people's land: I'd never persuade them to experiment with a cooperative. Apart from anything else, they don't trust each other, they don't trust you, or me, or God Almighty... Secondly, even if the conditions were such that I could accept your offer, I'd get myself in an endless legal wrangle and involve the Party, and neither the Party nor I would look good: it would be said, rightly, that we took advantage of an idiot... Thirdly, playing it clever with me is a waste of time: the person who can fool yours truly hasn't been born, and maybe never will be.'

'Who's the idiot?' Candido asked. 'Who's trying to play it clever?'

'You, my friend.'

'An idiot, who's trying to play it clever... Why, in what way?'

'You know perfectly well why and in what way.'

'I swear to you I don't know and don't understand.' And he said this in a tone of such desperation that the secretary not only began to suspect that he really didn't know and didn't under-stand but was also certain now that he really was an idiot.

'Don't you know that your relatives have started a legal action to have you disqualified on the grounds of incompetence?'

'What does that mean?'

'It means they want to take everything you have away from you.'

'I didn't know,' Candido said.

'If you didn't know, that's one thing,' said the secretary. 'But if you did know, and you came here to trap the Party and me into taking up your case against your relatives, defending you from them, arguing that you're still mentally sound, then that's another matter entirely, and you were wrong to do it.'

'I didn't know,' Candido said. 'And I'm sorry: but only because I've wasted your time, not because I tried to fool you.'

He went to see Don Antonio and told him everything. Don Antonio was furious: with the secretary, and even more so with Candido's relatives. But Candido was smarting more from the fact that the secretary had thought him capable of plotting a deception than from the fact that his relatives were trying, in their own way and, of course, for their own benefit, to find a solution to the problem he himself faced: that of freeing himself of his lands and property. He had developed a passion for the land, had worked on it: but without any sense of property, of possession; as if cultivating the land as best he could, making it more productive, better organised, more clearly defined, was a question of leading a better life and had nothing to do with revenue, with money. Something that was like love. Like his love for Paola. And now that Paola was gone, that everyday work of his seemed to him to have become debased: it was effort, nothing but effort, in the unchanging cycle of the seasons; just as it had always been for the peasants, who were never content, who were always cursing the rain or the sun, the hail or the frost, the phylloxera that attacked the vines or the black sickness that attacked the corn. And what the countryside presented every day to the peasants was the truest allegory of life: an effort that was every day undermined, and often destroyed; diseases that broke out invisibly and spread inexorably. And even those diseases, and the names the peasants gave them, were an allegory of life: the black sickness, the white sickness, the red sickness.

Don Antonio did not like Candido's indifference to his relatives' manoeuvres to have him disqualified on the grounds of incompetence. He could not understand how anyone could be so calm at the thought of having his property taken from him – however unjust the idea of property was, and however unjust the laws that guaranteed it... And, what was more, with a petition stating that he was mentally unstable. He therefore lost no time in investigating these tactics: which of Candido's relatives were behind them; what was being put forward to support the petition; who the lawyer was and who the judge; how far the procedure had gone in the legal labyrinth and what the judge thought of it. And within a few days he had found out all there was to know.

Candido's father's brothers and sisters had always hoped, as we know, to lay their hands on the property left by their brother: as if to carry out Francesco Maria Munafò's wish to disinherit Candido, which he would certainly have done himself if he had had time. But in the beginning, the general had been on Candido's side and had stood in their way, and the general was a man with powerful contacts, thanks both to a past that was not a past, and to a present that resembled the past. When the general had become disgusted with Candido, and Concetta had gone, to be replaced by that woman, their hopes had revived. But then Candido had joined the Communist Party, and that had stopped them in their tracks again, because the Party was sure to protect and assist him.

Candido's expulsion from the Party had been a signal to them that the way was clear. They sounded out the feelings of the general and Concetta: but the general did not even want to hear about Candido; while Concetta did not want to hear about him and talked about him: to her, he was a wretch, who, after she had devoted twenty years of love and sacrifice to him, was now heading for a wretched end. Nor did they neglect to sound out public opinion; which was, unanimously, this: that a woman like Paola *would eat him alive*: both with her *ars amandi*, in which she was undoubtedly very expert, and with her greed for money, which in a woman like her was sure to be very strong and ruthless. But while they were preparing the petition, Paola had left:

and, as everyone knew she had left when Candido was out of the house, and had been laden with luggage, the suspicion that that woman was robbing Candido became a certainty that she had robbed him.

Don Antonio even managed to get hold of a copy of the petition. As a general proof of Candido's mental instability, they put forward two facts which, by wanting to be subtle, actually contradicted one another: that, as a major landowner he had joined the Communist Party, which, as is well known, wants to give the land to the peasants; and that, after about a year, thanks to his exhibitionist obsession with giving away his own land as a gift, he had very wisely been expelled from the Party. There followed some more specific proofs: including such elements as his offer to donate to the town a substantial piece of land, valued at several million lire; the crazy amount of money he had spent on the land to bring about some very arguable improvements; and his cohabitation with a woman of unknown extraction who had had a very humble position in his grandfather's house: a cohabitation considered scandalous by the woman who had raised him (Concetta Munisteri, fifty-one years old, now in the service of Deputy Arturo Cressi: to be heard as a witness), and disapproved of by his grandfather (Deputy Arturo Cressi: also to be heard as a witness), a cohabitation that had ended with the woman leaving the Munafò house and presumably – as everyone in town presumed – taking with her objects of value from the Munafò inheritance.

'Great,' Candido said. 'With a petition like this, they're bound to get the land from me.'

How Candido spoke to a judge and a psychiatrist;
and the judgement that ensued.

Uncles and aunts, the aunts with their husbands, were sitting lined up in the judge's antechamber. Six, plus their lawyer: in that little room, it was a crowd. Candido greeted them cheerfully. Mistrusting that cheerfulness, they replied coldly. But one of the aunts did add, 'We're doing it for your good.' Candido replied, 'I know,' thinking that the aunt really believed that, and the others, too. So many things are done for other people's good which become other people's harm, and your own. Example: Paola had left. Example: these people wanted to save his property for him, or, if not save them for him, save them. His property, the Munafò inheritance: a kind of abstraction over which they would subsequently tear each other apart.

They were the first to be called into the judge's chambers. They rushed in, pushing and shoving, almost as if there might not be enough room for everyone and the last ones were afraid they would be left outside. They were in there for almost an hour, and came out looking less gloomy, almost happy; and the happiest of all was their lawyer. They said goodbye to Candido and swarmed out. From the door of the judge's chambers, the clerk of the court called, 'Candido Munafò' and Candido crossed the threshold of the chambers. The judge was sitting behind a desk. He had a hard face with an unnatural smile pasted on it, thick black hair and a low forehead. On his right, but as if apart from him, sat a very thin man with wild eyes, constantly running his hand nervously through his ruffled hair. Behind a smaller desk, the clerk of the court.

The judge half stood to shake Candido's hand, and introduced the man on his right as 'Professor Palicatti'. By way of greeting, the professor blinked. The judge gestured to Candido to sit down, and he did so, facing the two men. The judge was looking at him closely, Professor Palicatti was staring at him with remote, lifeless eyes.

'So...' the judge began. 'So...' He shifted a few papers, touched his pens and pencils, seemed to find in them the words he needed to get to the point. 'So, as you know, your relatives want to have you disqualified on the grounds of incompetence... What do you say to that?'

'Nothing: it's up to you to say something.'

'Right: it's up to me to say something... Professor Palicatti and I... Professor Palicatti,' he explained, 'is a psychiatrist.'

'Ah,' Candido said. He had not expected a psychiatrist to be involved, although he should have.

'So,' the judge went on, 'you have nothing to say about this action of your relatives to have you disqualified.'

'I'd say it was madness on their part to take on the responsibility of maintaining my property.'

'Madness, you say.' The judge seemed satisfied. 'Madness... I see... What do you think, Professor Palicatti?'

The professor raised his right hand in a gesture that might have been one of condemnation, absolution, expectation, or indifference.

'In other words,' the judge quickly resumed, 'you don't find your relatives' attempts to take your inheritance away from you reprehensible.'

'From a personal, selfish point of view, I even consider it a good deed.'

'You hear?' the judge asked the professor. His satisfaction now manifested itself in a sneer.

'I hear, I hear,' the professor said, a touch irritably.

'But in that case,' asked the judge, 'why haven't you, of your own free will, and without letting it come to this,' he waved his hand over the papers he had in front of him as if to liquidise them, 'handed over the administration, maintenance and protection of your inheritance to your relatives?'

'They never asked me. And besides, I thought it would have been asking too much of them.'

'Ah, asking too much... I see...' He cast a questioning glance at the professor but immediately, encountering a blank stare, looked away again.

'And besides,' Candido added, 'as long as there's the law and they turned to the law, it's better to do things by the rules, according to the law, according to justice.'

'According to the law, according to justice...' said the judge. 'Nice, very nice.' For a moment he was lost in thought, as if infatuated with the beauty of those two words, those two ideas: law and justice. Then he said, 'As far as I'm concerned, that's all... Professor, do you have any questions to ask our friend?' The expression 'our friend', and the tone in which he uttered it, was a clear indication to Candido that the judge already considered him fully deserving of the disqualification his relatives had asked for.

'Many questions,' said the professor.

'Go ahead,' said the judge.

'Well,' said the professor, 'I'd like to know something about your expulsion from the Communist Party.'

Candido told the story in an orderly manner.

'Personally,' the professor said when Candido had finished, 'it's the Communist Party I would disqualify.'

'What do you mean?' the judge said in surprise. 'Aren't you a Communist?'

'I am,' said the professor, 'but let's say a little *refoulé*.'

'Oh, dear...' the judge said, anxiously. 'Chinese?'

'Not exactly... But don't worry. I'll pass this case to my colleague, who's a Social Democrat.... A conscientious man, a very good doctor... But Signor Munafò will still have to go to hospital for a few days: for observation... I can't, off the top of my head, just – '

'All right, all right...' the judge cut in. 'We'll talk about it now... In the meantime, Signor Munafò, you can go.'

And so it was that Candido spent two days in an asylum. He was well treated, but what drove him mad was seeing how the others were treated. And even though he did not actually go mad, that good, conscientious Social Democrat doctor did certify him as mentally unstable, just as the judge, his relatives and he himself had expected.

**How Candido's relatives threw him a party
to reward him for the way he had behaved with
the judge and the doctors; and how they then
had further problems because of that party.**

Of the events surrounding his disqualification, two remained
indelibly etched in Candido's memory: Professor Palicatti's re-
linquishment of the case and the sudden warm affection his
relatives showed him once the disqualification had been ruled
on.

Professor Palicatti was the first example Candido had ever
come across of a Communist to the left of the Communists. He
had heard they existed, but had never met one. The nonchalance
with which the professor, having made a little joke about the
Communist Party and aroused the judge's suspicion, had washed
his hands of making any judgement in science and conscience,
had impressed him greatly. He had seen him again at the hospital,
and had gone up to him and let himself be recognised. 'Ah, yes,'
the professor had said, 'I remember...' As if five years rather than
five days had passed since they had met in the judge's chambers.
'But my dear friend, I always wash my hands of these sordid
cases... Money, property: do you think I care whether you keep
them or they go to your relatives?' And he walked off, furiously
ruffling his hair. Candido stood there stunned, especially by that
'dear friend' which had rather echoed the judge's words.

As for Candido's relatives, it seemed to him that the way he
had consented to their petition, and had even confirmed it to the
judge and the doctor as being justified, had convinced them that
he liked them, and so, feeling remorse at the fact that they had
not liked him in all those years, they were now very anxious
to do well by him. When Candido told them about his decision
to leave, and perhaps never return (a decision which in their
hearts they approved enthusiastically and hoped would last),

they decided to focus and demonstrate all the affection they felt they owed him for the past, and would have liked to show him in the future, in a big family gathering; almost a party.

Candido barely knew these relatives of his who now liked him so much. Two aunts, two uncles, the aunts' husbands, the uncles' wives, and a dozen cousins, male and female. And there were others, whose relationship to him was more distant. Candido confused the names and the faces, and suffered through much of the evening. But at last, from out of that crowd which was like a pack of cards being constantly reshuffled, there emerged the court card that he could not confuse with any other, the card he could trust, as always happens to the shy and the lost who find themselves in the middle of a large group of people they do not know. His cousin Francesca, his Aunt Amelia's daughter. She couldn't be called beautiful, but she had a gleam in her eyes and a lovely smile. She was also intelligent and lively, quick with jokes and cutting remarks. She attached herself to Candido, and Candido to her, for the rest of the evening, in other words, until dawn.

When the time came to say goodbye, Francesca said to Candido, 'I want to come with you.' She said it with a smile, as if it was a joke, as if ready to withdraw it and flee; but there was a tremulous, plangent note in her voice.

'Where?' Candido asked.

'Anywhere.' And this she said with a serious, determined look on her face.

By the time Candido returned home, he wondered if he was falling in love or had already fallen in love. He therefore decided to bring forward his departure. But the next day, as he was riding out into the country, he suddenly heard the roar of another motorbike coming up behind him. Francesca was riding on his left, her face pale and determined, her hair blowing in the wind. 'I love you,' she cried. 'So do I,' Candido cried.

They spent a couple of hours together, walking through the countryside. And a week later they left together.

For Francesca's parents, for Francesca's and Candido's aunts and uncles, for all the relatives, this was a defeat and a sign of breakdown. At first, everyone was against Candido. He had brought misfortune to the Munafò family from the day he was born; they would have done better not to get involved with him and his property; someone like him, who had been born badly and had lived worse, could only corrupt and destroy everything good and beautiful... Then opinions began to differ, and sides to form. Francesca's parents began to hope that the union of their daughter with Candido would be legalised and sanctified in marriage: and consequently that the disqualification they had worked so hard to obtain would be lifted. But the others were of a different opinion, they did not want to drop the guardianship of the properties. Quarrels started. There were a few fights. Strong enmities were established.

Candido and Francesca learned something of all this: but as if it were news from a distant world, and a remote time.

How Candido and Francesca travelled; and how they spent a long time in Turin.

Candido still had some money, although he had spent a lot of it on his land. The money accumulated by the avaricious comes out on many sides, through many holes: and it takes the type of avarice known as generosity for it to disperse quickly on many sides. Candido had spent a lot: wisely, even though his spending had been deemed mad in the verdict of disqualification; and he still had some money left. He had already decided, before meeting Francesca, to spend it on travelling, and Francesca agreed with the idea. After that they could think about work.

Francesca had always wanted to go to Spain, Candido to France. They went to Spain and France. Then to Egypt, Persia and Israel. But everything always seemed deteriorated compared with what they had imagined. The only places that did not disappoint them were Barcelona, because of the people, and Paris, because of everything. But the best part of their journey was loving each other and making love: as if the essence of the places again became imagination in their bodies: as if the imagination of those places, or the memory, were their very bodies.

They did not have any adventures, mishaps or setbacks. Loving each other and loving everybody – the waiters, the drivers, the guides, the tramps, the children in the poorer quarters, the Arabs, the Jews – they felt that they were loved by everybody. They also witnessed things which they knew could and did happen, which, if they had read about them in a newspaper, would have disappeared without trace but which, by being seen, remained indelible and emblematic. In Madrid, at the celebrations for the anniversary of the civil war which Franco had won, next to the 'generalisimo' who looked as though he was solidified on a baroque tombstone (Candido recalled the photograph his grandfather kept in his bedroom) they saw, smiling down attentively at the military parade passing below, the ambassador from Mao's China. And in Cairo, as full of Russians as Rome was of Americans, in a café that was indeed full of Russians (technicians, it was said: they always went around in groups, with the gait and caution of a military patrol), they saw the police arrest a student because, as a waiter explained, he was suspected of being a Communist. Communist China paying tribute to a Fascist victory, Communist Russia helping a government that put Communists in prison: who knows how many of these contradictions, inconsistencies and absurdities there are in the world – Candido and Francesca told themselves – which elude us, which we do not see, which we would rather not see but have elude us. Because if we saw them, things would become simple, whereas we have a need to complicate them, to make complicated analyses, to find complicated causes, reasons and justifications for them. And when we do see them, they no longer have those justifications: let alone when we suffer them.

Returning to Italy, they travelled some more, trying to choose a city where they could settle and find work. Candido liked Milan, Francesca Turin. They decided to settle in Turin. Don Antonio recommended them to a priest who had left the priesthood and a priest who was about to leave the priesthood: the latter found work for Francesca in a kindergarten, the former for Candido in a machine shop. They went to live in the Via Garibaldi, which was full of Sicilians. It was as if they had come back home again. And they also came back to the Communist Party, thanks to the two priests. It was very different from the one in their town. The Communists here knew everything about Communism. But it was as if, by knowing everything, they ended up knowing nothing. In Sicily they knew nothing, and it was as if they knew everything.

Candido did not hide the story of his expulsion from the Party from the comrades in Turin, in fact he told it in great detail. Those who heard it commented that anything could and did happen down there in Sicily – even, unfortunately, in the Communist Party. Over time, they said, and, of course, with the consent of those who had expelled him, he would be re-admitted. But, over time, they began to be wary of him.

It all started one evening when they were talking about the danger of a coup d'état in Italy. They all believed it would happen and no one except Candido put forward the suggestion that it would fail. Some said that they had to be prepared to leave Italy, and almost everyone agreed. Candido asked, 'And where would you go?' Most replied that they would go to France; others to Canada and Australia. Then Candido asked – and also asked himself, since he, too, had thought, like most of them, of France – 'How come no one wants to go to the Soviet Union?' Some of them gave him black looks, others muttered under their breaths. 'Is it or isn't it a Socialist country?' he went on. Almost in unison they replied, 'Yes, of course… Obviously it's a Socialist country.' 'In that case,' Candido said, 'we ought to want to go there: if we are Socialists.' There was an icy silence; then, as though it was later than usual, even though it was in fact earlier than usual, they all got up and left. A few days later, Candido was told by a comrade who was more charitable than the others that, because of his remarks that evening, the comrades now considered him a provocateur. And after that, the more he tried to explain, to clarify matters, the more the others bristled and withdrew into their mistrust. Candido felt saddened and troubled. Until one evening, returning from one of these meetings, Francesca asked, 'And what if they're just idiots?' And that was the beginning of his liberation, his cure.

Meanwhile, Turin was becoming an increasingly grim place. It was as if the city were cut vaguely in two, as if there were some fluid dividing line down the middle: two cities laying siege to one another, neurotically, unable to recognise one another's positions, defences, outposts, or Friesian and Trojan horses. The north and south of Italy scrambled around, madly trying to avoid each other and at the same time to strike blows at each other, both bottled up producing cars, a necessity that was surplus to requirements, something surplus to requirements that everyone thought necessary. Genuinely bottled up: thinking about the city, Candido was reminded of the image of two scorpions in a bottle which a famous American journalist had used to sum up the situation of the two nuclear powers, the Soviet Union and the United States of America. The north and south of Italy were also like two scorpions in a bottle – and the bottle was Turin.

He wrote to Don Antonio about the situation in Turin. Yes, Don Antonio replied, it was terrible: but the Piedmontese had wanted it that way, and it wouldn't last. But we Southerners are paying for it, retorted Candido. Yes, but after a while we'll break the bottle, replied Don Antonio. He had become a bit *gauchiste*, a bit Maoist, a bit May '68. But still within the Communist Party. Trying to overtake it on the Left, he said, was pure madness, infinite and circular: you found yourself on the Right without realising it. But, Candido asked, isn't it like being inside another bottle? Yes, replied Don Antonio, but not like a bottle of scorpions.

How Candido and Francesca visited Paris;
and how they decided to settle there.

They often went to Paris. Every time they had a holiday of more than four days: that way, excluding the hours spent on the train, they would have at least three full days there. They didn't have a car: living in a city that flooded the rest of Italy with cars, it had seemed almost natural to them not to buy one. And one of the reasons they loved Paris – apart from the fact that they loved love, loved literature, loved old, small things and old, small trades – was the fact that you could still walk there, still stroll, still dreamily stop and look at things. Only in Paris, for example, did they walk hand in hand; only in Paris did their pace assume a delightful slowness. In a word, they felt free there, liberated. And of course there was something mental, something literary in that: but there was also something in the spaces, in the rhythms of the architecture and the life that went on in those spaces, which fitted the idea, even the cliché, that you first had to get to know the city. It was a great city full of literary, libertarian and aphrodisiac myths, overlapping and merging: like the way that, in a nude by Courbet, you felt the interlude between one act of love and another, the Commune and the conversation with Baudelaire; but it was also a collection of little villages among which to choose, extract and experience the one that best suits us, the one in which we were born or where we have dreamed of living. Little villages which reflect each other and echo the great city: a great city that smells of the country, feeds off it, takes its breath from it, and echoes it through symbols. 'In front of the shops sat cats, waving their tails like flags. They were still, their eyes on the lookout, like guard dogs in front of baskets of green lettuces and yellow carrots, blue-tinged cabbages and pink radishes. The shops seemed like gardens... The café terraces bloomed with round tables on thin legs, and the waiters looked like gardeners, and when they poured coffee and milk into cups they seemed to be watering white flowerbeds. Along the sides of the streets were trees and kiosks, it was as if the trees were selling newspapers. In the shop windows, the goods danced in merry confusion, yet in a very precise and always superhuman order. The policemen strolled in the streets, yes, strolled, with capes over their right or left shoulders; and it was quite strange to think that such a garment was supposed to protect them from hail and rain. All the same, they wore them with an unwavering faith in the quality of the material or the goodness of the sky – who can know? They did not move like policemen, but like people who have nothing to do and time to see the world.' What Paris had been for Lieutenant Franz Tunda[7] in 1926 (an Austrian, displaced first by the war in Siberia, then by the peace in Europe) it still was for Candido and Francesca half a century later. And perhaps the city was no longer like that for those who had been born there and lived there, or for those who had known it before. 'Paris is no longer Paris': a common idea, put about by those who knew it well and by those who did not know it at all. But for them, Paris was still Paris.

And so they went there whenever they could; and always contemplated settling there. And since Candido often talked about it in the machine shop, one day a workmate of his, who was about to move to Paris to work in a machine shop owned by a relative, suggested that he should go, too: the work was assured, the pay was good; and Paris was Paris. He talked about it to Francesca. She was enthusiastic at first, but when she thought about it she grew worried: Candido would continue with his old job, but she would lose hers. And how could they live in Paris if she didn't also work and earn money?

They had just about resigned themselves to giving up, when Francesca, reading a book badly translated from French, and thinking about how badly translated it was, had an idea. She had never abandoned the French she had learned at the Institute of the Sacred Heart: in fact she had nurtured and improved it. She went to the Einaudi offices and asked if they would let her translate a book. Somewhat hesitantly, as if to keep her happy and get rid of her, they gave her a book called *Un rêve fait à Mantoue* to translate, as a trial run. Francesca skimmed through a few pages. The name of the author, Yves Bonnefoy, was almost like an omen. Bonnefoy:[8] good faith. But the people who had given her that to translate were not in good faith. It was a difficult text: it was obvious they wanted to discourage her, to see her return only to give back the book and drop the whole idea.

Francesca took the bit between her teeth and got down to work. It can even be said that she worked day and night. By the time she returned to the Einaudi offices, she knew everything about Bonnefoy it was possible to find out from the libraries in Turin, and had with her a translated chapter. They told her she had done a good job and could continue, and the translation would be published.

How Candido and Don Antonio wrote to each other; and how Don Antonio came to Paris.

Don Antonio approved of their move to Paris. He approved of almost anything that grew out of restlessness, anything that was an attempt to realise what you want or dream of. And he approved it with the melancholy of someone who, although a prisoner, does not envy the freedom that others enjoy, but only regrets that, at a certain point in his life, he has not seen that there was a possible escape, a possible freedom. 'I feel ever more a priest,' he wrote, 'and in that I am helped, a help I would rather have done without, by the evolution of the Party: an evolution I don't disapprove of, don't dispute (a Marxism that doesn't evolve, that doesn't adapt to reality, that isn't flexible, would be paralysis, a negation of itself) except in relation to myself, to this part of myself that finds it hard to die and would like to be helped to die by other people... Perhaps I'll get married... Perhaps I'll become a priest again...' Sometimes he was swept by waves of Leftism, and would lambaste the Party: 'The Party of the working class! And what's more, or rather, what's less, of the employed working class! As if the employed working class, precisely because it's employed, precisely because it doesn't have to worry about employment, weren't susceptible to corruption if placed, as it in fact is, in a corrupt social fabric... It is only from the unemployed and the students, university being the vast antechamber of revolution, that there might come, I don't say the revolution, which has now been postponed indefinitely, but the strength for a real, effective change in Italian society... But the Party doesn't want to hear about the unemployed and the students, especially as the un-employed and the students don't want to know anything about the Party. When a good Communist hears the word *students*, he takes out his revolver, like Doctor Goebbels when he heard the word *culture*. But I'm not a good Communist…' But sometimes he, too, took out his revolver: 'What the student *gauchistes* haven't understood (not that they ever could, being children of the bourgeoisie) is that you can't tell the worker who at last has something to eat that, just because he has something to eat, he's running the risk of not being sufficiently revolutionary. Giving up its mess of pottage for the revolutionary birthright doesn't seem a sensible idea to the working class; and so in the friend who turns up on the Left it detects, beneath the revolutionary language, the red flags and the language of Lenin, the old enemy who up until yesterday turned up only on the Right.' Then he would again get angry with the Party: 'Yesterday I met a young man who had just come back from spending four months in Moscow. He had been sent there by the Party to take lessons in Marxism-Leninism: in other words, Stalinism. Exactly the same thing they were doing twenty years ago. Today I asked Deputy Di Sales about it: he said he knew nothing about it, in fact he didn't think it was possible. I told him the young man's name, and described him. He knew him, but didn't know he had been sent to Moscow. He made an uninhibited crack. "Maybe," he said, "they only send the most stupid people to that school." "Yes," I replied, "that's quite possible, since even in the Party the future belongs to the stupid…" He smiled sadly: maybe he's convinced that the future belongs to the stupid, after all, he has been rather left to one side lately. Now when two Communists meet (only two, no more than that) they talk about the Soviet Union, the Party and certain men in the Party with the same uninhibitedness and freedom with which priests talk among themselves about the Pope, the Roman curia, the bishop's curia… But what this story of the young man sent to school in Russia tells me is that all the fine talk about euro-Communism, Italian Communism, emancipation from the Soviet Union, is just that: fine talk…' But a few months later: 'To liquidate the myth of Stalin was already a great mistake; liquidating the myth of the Soviet Union is even worse. And besides, I don't believe the Soviet Union is a myth (although it still is for the old grass-roots Communists), certainly not an empty one, nor do I believe the Soviet Union is really a fascist country, as some Communists say, even though they still go there for medical treatment or endless junkets: the revolution did take place...'

In his letters, Candido told him about Paris, his life there with Francesca, the things they saw: but Don Antonio never wrote about anything except the Party, his own Communism, and how Communist the Communist Party was or wasn't. Every time, what he said was a truth. After a while, Candido tried to put all these truths together. They wouldn't go: it was as if they bubbled up and overflowed... He wrote to Don Antonio: 'I reread your letters: there are so many truths, and all so different from each other, that a man can't contain them all, and nor can a party.' Don Antonio replied: 'A party can't contain them all: in fact, the Communist Party is selecting the worst. But the Left can, and the man of the Left... These many truths, which absolutely have to go together, constitute the drama of the man of the Left, and of the Left itself. And the Communist Party has to live through them all again, if it doesn't want to leave the Left... It's like the problem of free will and predestination for a Catholic: two truths that must coexist.' Candido, who did not know much about the problem of free will and predestination, replied: 'What if the sum of all these truths were a great lie? It's a simple question, and there may be a simple answer to it.'

Don Antonio replied: 'We'll talk about that when I come to Paris.' He had been saying, ever since they had moved there, that he would come to Paris for a trip. And in August 1977, after putting it off from one month to the next, from one year to the next, he finally came. Candido and Francesca went to meet him at the Gare de Lyon. He had aged a lot, and was very exhausted from the journey and a bit bewildered. But on the taxi ride from the Gare de Lyon to the hotel in Saint-Germain they had booked for him, just reading the names of the streets and bridges and seeing the Seine and Notre Dame, he perked up, and went back to being the lively, curious, tireless Don Antonio of ten years earlier.

How Candido met his mother,
and the evening they spent together; and how,
that evening, Candido finally felt happy.

'In the evening I went to Lipp's.' It was like a musical theme, a song, which surfaced in Don Antonio every time he passed the place; and he passed it more than once a day, as it was near his hotel. 'In the evening I went to Lipp's.' Hemingway or Fitzgerald? Probably Hemingway, *A Moveable Feast*.

One day, Candido was with him when, instead of repeating it mentally, he said the sentence in a low voice. 'In the evening I went to Lipp's.' And Candido said, 'We'll go there this evening... Or even this afternoon, because it's difficult to get a seat in the evening.'

They went there in the afternoon. All the tables were taken, and they had to wait for one to be free. Finally they got one in a corner. It was a bit uncomfortable for the three of them: but Don Antonio, Candido understood, wanted to mark that place down as having been visited, on the map of legendary Parisian places which he had drawn up for himself in all those years of reading.

Francesca and Candido asked for coffee and Don Antonio an *armagnac*: both because he couldn't take more than a sip of the coffee they made in Paris, and because in Paris he wanted to eat and drink according to literature.

Armagnac, then. Or *pastis*. Or *calvados*. A bold homage to literature for an almost teetotal Sicilian accustomed to drinking half a glass of red wine with his lunch and dinner, like almost all Sicilians.

They talked about Hemingway and Fitzgerald, and Americans in Paris, and the American writers Don Antonio had read during the years of Fascism, when they had all seemed very great writers to him: Candido and Francesca had also read them, but casually and even impatiently. At the next table was an American couple. There was no mistaking the fact that they were American. The man had neatly combed snow-white hair, a full, pink face, glasses with thin metal rims, and a cigar between his teeth; the woman had an old face, hair so white it was almost purple, large heavy glasses shaped like a butterfly, and a slender, youthful figure. There was something tired, bored, sleepy about the man, in contrast with the energetic volubility with which the woman was talking and moving her hands. Only American women are so old and at the same time so young; and only American men have that air of postprandial drowsiness – almost to the point of nausea – when they are with their spouses.

When Francesca, Don Antonio and Candido sat down at the table next to theirs, she was talking and her husband was nodding his head almost rhythmically. Then she fell silent, apparently intent on catching what the three newcomers were saying. After a while, she turned to them and asked in Italian, 'Are you Italian?' Francesca, Don Antonio and Candido said yes. 'I'm Italian, too,' the American woman said. She did not seem to have anything more to say; but after having looked closely at them for a long time the woman asked, 'Are you Sicilian?' When they replied in the affirmative, she turned to her husband and emitted a long 'Oh!' of wonder and happiness, the typical American 'Oh!' which is heard winding its way, like a thread uniting them, through the crowd at the fireworks display on the Seine on the fourteenth of July, each time a rocket lights up the sky. 'I'm Sicilian, too,' she said, and again looked at them with a hesitant, anxious expression, as if the question she wanted to ask, which she was about to ask, might well reveal the card of destiny.

She finally made up her mind to ask it. 'From what town?'

Don Antonio told her the name of their town.

She stood up, shaking with emotion, her hand on her chest as if to stop her heart from pounding. Speaking to Don Antonio but looking at Candido, she said, 'You're the archpriest Lepanto; and you...' But Candido had already guessed in the last few seconds that this woman was his mother.

A scene out of a soap opera followed, in the middle of Lipp's, which the approach of a waiter brought to an end. They paid and left. Signora Maria Grazia took off her big butterfly glasses and wiped away her tears. Tenderly supporting her and repeating her name – 'Grace, Grace' – her husband looked at the three of them with a reproving air, as if they were guilty of an intrusion that was spoiling their vacation.

Grace calmed down. Pointing to her husband, she said to Candido, 'This is...' Perhaps she was about to say *your father*, perhaps *my husband*. She turned red, and a faraway look came into her eyes. After a while she said, 'This is Amleto.' Amleto shook hands warmly with Candido, Francesca, Don Antonio, asking each of them in Italian, 'How are you?' All three replied that they were fine.

It was Grace and Amleto's last evening in Paris: they were leaving the following day, and Amleto could not put off their departure. What a pity that they had met only on their last evening. Candido was living in Paris, they had been here for two weeks: how great it would have been if they had met earlier! Anyway, that evening they would spend together. Ceremoniously, Amleto invited the three of them to dinner in a famous restaurant.

As they walked through Paris, they talked about their town (which even Amleto considered somewhat as his: after all, he had run it for a few months, and he had met the love of his life there), about Sicily, Italy, Europe. Unwittingly, they avoided talking about their lives. But they were thinking about it, especially the son and the mother: and both made vain gestures towards love and remorse. If they had been alone, they would have had nothing to say to each other, or very little. Fortunately, Don Antonio and Amleto were there, and they had started talking politics.

'After thirty-four years –' Don Antonio began.

'Your age,' Grace cut in, looking tenderly at Candido.

'After thirty-four years,' Don Antonio resumed, 'perhaps I can ask you a question I hope you won't think indiscreet.'

'Go ahead,' Amleto said.

'Well, the question is this: why, when you'd barely been in our town for a few days, did you choose the worst people for public office? Were they just there when you arrived, or had you been told who they were beforehand?'

'Were they the worst?' Amleto asked, with a smile.

'Yes, they were… Of course, I'm only asking the question now out of, let's say, historical curiosity, I'm not trying to score points.'

'I'll answer you, I don't think I'm still sworn to secrecy. I didn't choose them. When they sent me to your town, they gave me a list of the people I had to trust… Had to: in other words, it was an order.' And, very formally, he added, 'I'm sorry.'

'We're even sorrier,' Don Antonio said. 'Anyway, I always suspected it. I mean, that you arrived with a list of Mafia bosses in your pocket.'

'I can tell you, I also suspected they'd given me a list of Mafiosi… But look, we were at war…'

They talked about war, about peace, and about Germany. Grace and Amleto had spent two months touring around Europe, and the only country that hadn't disappointed them was Germany. 'Europe,' said Amleto, 'has become an orphanage: De Gaulle's orphans, Franco's orphans, Salazar's orphans; and in Italy, the orphans of the Communist Party… Only the Germans have a father, even if he's a ghost.'

'A ghost as Hamlet's father was for Hamlet,' said Don Antonio.

Amleto smiled at this reminder of Hamlet. 'But,' he said, 'since Sartre seems to be the only person in Europe who's worried about it, do you think we Americans should worry about it? On the contrary, I think – '

They were already at the restaurant. 'Enough with the politics,' Grace interrupted, 'let's think about dinner.' Amleto knew about wines: he chose them, and submitted his choice to the others' judgement, but none of them knew as much as he did.

They ate well. Amleto and Don Antonio drank copiously, the others in moderation.

They walked Grace and Amleto to their hotel. Grace told Candido and Francesca that they should move to America. 'We'll come one of these days,' Candido said. 'But not to stay. I want to stay here…. Here, you can feel that something is about to finish and something else is about to start: I like seeing what has to finish actually finish.' As she embraced him one last time, his mother thought, 'He's a monster,' but through her tears she said, 'In America there's everything. I'll wait for you.'

Candido, Francesca and Don Antonio walked down the Champs-Elysées. The night was very mild. They decided to walk across Paris, since the next day was Sunday. Those good wines had made Don Antonio not exactly merry, but freer and more fanciful. He said, 'You're right, it's true: here you feel that something is ending: and it's a nice feeling… In Sicily, nothing is ending, nothing ever ends…' He almost sobbed.

They passed Maillol's statues: Don Antonio contemplated sleeping next to one of those bronze women. 'Sleeping,' he said, 'sleeping chastely: the chastest sleep of my life.' He spoke for a long time about chastity, in the Latin of the Holy Fathers.

They crossed the Pont Saint-Michel, and Don Antonio, almost preaching, began, 'Here, in 1968, in the month of May –'

'Were they our grandfathers or our grandchildren?' Candido cut in.

'A disturbing question,' Don Antonio said. And he fell silent, lost in thought, muttering.

From the *quai*, they took the Rue de Seine. In front of the statue of Voltaire, Don Antonio stopped, grabbed hold of the signpost, and bowed his head. It seemed as if he had started praying. 'This is our father,' he cried, 'this is our true father.'

Gently but firmly, Candido prised him free of the signpost and, supporting him, dragged him away. 'Let's not start again about fathers,' he said. He himself, he thought, was the son of fortune; and he felt happy.

Author's note

Montesquieu says that 'an original work almost always gives birth to five or six hundred others, which use the original more or less the way surveyors use their formulas.' I don't know if *Candide* has served as a formula for five or six hundred other books. I don't think so, unfortunately: we might not have had so much boring literature. However, whether this book of mine is the first or the six hundredth, I have tried to use that formula. But I don't feel that I have succeeded, I think this book is very much like my other books. It isn't possible any longer to recapture the same speed and lightness: even I, as someone who tries never to bore his readers, can't do that. Whatever the result, at least the intention was good: I did try to be fast and light. But our times are heavy, very heavy.

Notes

1. The word candido has two meanings in Italian: both 'innocent' and 'snow-white' – the latter explaining the lawyer Munafò's choice of name.
2. Literally meaning 'in the heart', *in pectore* is used to refer to something kept undisclosed. Its use originated in the Roman Catholic Church to describe the manner in which the Pope keeps secret his choice of newly-appointed Cardinal.
3. Pietro Badoglio (1871–1956), was an Italian soldier and politician. A member of the Fascist Party, he was briefly named Prime Minister of Italy following the Mussolini's removal from power in 1943.
4. Antonio Gramsci (1891–1937) was an Italian philosopher and is considered a prominent figure in the history of Marxist theory. A founding member of and, for a time, the leader of the Communist Party of Italy, he was imprisoned by Mussolini's Fascist regime.
5. Palmiro Togliatti (1893–1964), was leader of the Italian Communist Party from 1927 until 1964.
6. Arnobius of Sicca (d. c. 330) was a rhetorician who, having converted to Christianity, wrote a work of Christian apology in seven volumes entitled *Adversus Nationes*.
7. Franz Tunda is the hero of a novel by Joseph Roth, *Flight Without End*. An Austrian officer imprisoned in Siberia as a Russian prisoner of war, Tunda roams through Europe, including Paris, as he makes his way back from Siberia to Vienna.
8. Yves Bonnefoy is a French poet. He was born in 1923 in Tours and became a major figure in post-war literature.

Biographical note

Leonardo Sciascia was born in 1921 in Racalmuto, Sicily. Interested in writing from a young age, the author became a primary school teacher in 1941, and married Maria Andronico in 1944, with whom he was to have two daughters.

Heavily influenced by Sicilian life, Sciascia was a prolific writer not only of novels but also of poetry, drama and short stories. He is perhaps best known today for his crime novels such as *The Day of the Owl* and *Equal Danger*. Being part of the House of Deputies responsible for the investigation into Aldo Moro's kidnapping gave him the experience which enabled him to write *The Moro Affair*. His books examine, sometimes controversially, the nature of justice and politics, dealing in particular with the influence of the Mafia on Sicilian life.

Sciascia was elected as a councillor in Sicily in 1975 but resigned in 1977 in protest at the Communist Party's dealings with the Christian Democrats. He was later elected a deputy in the National Assembly and eventually became a member of the European Parliament.

A Simple Story came out in bookshops on the very day of his death in 1989.

Howard Curtis lives and works in London. He has translated many books from French and Italian, mostly fiction, including *The Way of the Kings* by André Malraux, *A Private Affair* by Beppe Fenoglio, *The Turn* by Luigi Pirandello, *The Vendetta* by Honoré de Balzac and *Three Tales* by Gustave Flaubert all published by Hesperus Press. His translation of Edoardo Albinati's *Coming Back*, also published by Hesperus Press, won the 2004 John Florio Prize for Italian Translation.